Magpies

Short Stories from Wales

Edited by
Robert Nisbet

First Impression—2000

ISBN 1 85902 851 9

© The authors

All rights reserved. No part of this book may be reproduced, stored in a retrieval system, or transmitted in any form or by any means, electronic, electrostatic, magnetic tape, mechanical, photocopying, recording or otherwise, without permission in writing from the publishers, Gomer Press, Llandysul, Ceredigion, Wales.

This volume is published with the support of the
Arts Council of Wales.

Printed in Wales at
Gomer Press, Llandysul, Ceredigion SA44 4QL

Contents

Acknowledgements	6
Editor's Foreword	7

GLENDA BEAGAN
Green Eggs and Larches	9
My Friend of the Earth	15
Foxy	21

LEONORA BRITO
Moonbeam Kisses	30
Mama's Baby (Papa's Maybe)	37

GILLIAN CLARKE
A Field of Hay	57
The Blue Man	62
Honey	68

JO HUGHES
Too Perfect	81
Magpie	88
Running Away with the Hairdresser	94

MIKE JENKINS
Some Kind o' Beginning	99
Wanting to Belong	106
Allotment for Memories	115

CATHERINE MERRIMAN
Aberrance in the Emotional Spectrum	119
Delivery	134

ROBERT NISBET
Jam Jars of Seaweed and Dreams of Love	149
Entertaining Sally Ann	158
An April Story	167

Biographical Notes	175

Acknowledgements

Some of these stories were first published and broadcast by the following: Alun Books; Parthian Books; Planet Books; Seren Books; *Cambrensis*; *New Welsh Review*; *Social Care Education*; BBC Radio 4; BBC Radio Wales; *The Slate*: BBC Wales TV.

Jo Hughes' story, *Running Away with the Hairdresser*, is based on a 1995 painting of the same title by Kevin Sinnott (collection: National Museums and Galleries of Wales).

Editor's Foreword

I like to think that the stories appearing here represent a rich selection of the best short fiction which has been written, and is still being written, in the English language in Wales in the last decade or so of the twentieth century. The stories have emerged from a range of sources: some have come along the regulation pathway of collections, anthologies and magazines, while many of them are appearing here for the first time.

This eclecticism is deliberate. I feel that some of the previously-collected stories (comprising some of the work by Glenda Beagan, Mike Jenkins and Leonora Brito) have established themselves as classics of their kind. Yet in the sifting through of the many manuscripts sent me, I have encountered many fresh pleasures: the relatively little-known short fiction of Gillian Clarke; some increasingly venturesome new work by Catherine Merriman; the distinctive voice to be found in the writing of Jo Hughes.

The rationale behind the anthology is that a great deal has indeed been written in the short story form in Wales recently and that a number of extremely interesting writers has emerged, often with one or more impressive collections, or with a number of anthology appearances. However, whereas most anthologies tend to work to a format of twenty-stories-by-twenty-writers, I felt it a good idea to seek to confine this book to the very best of those we have writing at the present time and to offer these writers a space of about ten thousand words, in which they might show their paces and which might enable readers new (or comparatively new) to the field of Welsh short fiction in English a chance to enjoy a generous sample of some of these practitioners. As a result, I have drawn upon a few of these earlier collections, but have included also quite a number of stories which are appearing in book form for the first time.

The title of this volume might then have been *Seven Contemporary Writers of Welsh Short Fiction in English*, or something equally cumbersome. I have opted instead to call the book *Magpies*, although my reasons for doing so may owe a little more to the fancy than to the imagination. To me, a short story writer is like a magpie, someone who can pick unerringly on little moments of brightness, small aesthetic objects, the very stuff of the short story form. We hope you enjoy this collection of nineteen such bright objects by seven such magpies.

Robert Nisbet

GLENDA BEAGAN

Green Eggs and Larches

God was watching.

It seemed to the child, travelling in the slumbery warmth of the bus down lanes deep with rabbits and herb robert, that up there was a place God would choose to live.

There were larches. Their shapes were miracles, wind-whittled, they cowered and hunched but were strong too, like old warriors. Or wizards, perhaps.

There was something plain and fierce about those shapes, the spirits of high places. And from up there you had the sense of being able to feel free and apart, the way God must feel she supposed. Looking down was a good feeling. All the sandbanks in the estuary, the treacherous quicks and whirlpools looked small and tame, the water around them milky, or palest green like an opal. It was a trick of distance and light.

'Are we nearly there now?' she kept asking.

Perhaps the journey was the best bit. She wasn't sure she really liked Aunty Ellie. She was a tall big-boned woman, and not at all smiling, even when you first got there and were stood waiting for her to come to the door, in the porch with the tiles of lilies on the walls and the scraper for boots and shoes. It was shaped like a dolphin but with spikes.

Ellie's clothes smelled of mothballs (camphor, mam said it was) and her breath smelt of peppermints. She had furrowed elbows, the lines on them just like tramlines. Her arms were strong-looking, very muscular, because she has to do a man's work, mam told her, and her hands were broad and strong. But it was her face that was frightening, a bit. She had a very staring look even if she wasn't staring. It was the sort of face that knew everything. The child felt that there was nothing you could hide from her. It was as if she already knew all there was to know about you and was disappointed.

So why did she like to go?

Well, there was the journey for a start. And it was somewhere special and different, quite unlike home, their house in Pretoria Terrace with only a thin strip at the back for a garden. Up at Ellie's there was so much space and sky.

They had to change buses to get there and there was half an hour to wait in between. To pass the time they went to the milk-bar on the corner opposite the bus station. Mam would have coffee and she would have a milkshake, lime or raspberry and very frothy, and they would sit in the window if they could.

There was a pub on the other corner, The Volunteer, a disreputable place mam said, with pillars and a kind of verandah outside where the Teddy Boys stood. They all had sleeked black hair and they were all tall and thin and looked like turkeys, the way they strutted about that is, not their shapes.

She had seen turkeys up at Ellie's, being fattened up for Christmas. Most had been ordinary black, with just those bits of red for their combs and wattles. But there was also a pair of what Ellie called her beauties, and they could have been birds of paradise. They were white and gold and red, very noisy and proud. But for all their twirling they'd go the same way as the rest, Ellie'd said with a glint about her.

While mam and Ellie were catching up with their news in the parlour with the harmonium and the pictures of Roman ladies in long white dresses, she went exploring up the still steep hill as far as the larches where God lived.

It was a game she played, imagining places for God to live in, high places they were of course, always. Last time, though, she was restless a bit, and the wind too cold to hang about in. 'Sometimes,' Ellie said, 'the tail end of March is the coldest there is.' It was the east wind that came biting and hissing in the browned old needles of the larch trees, but there were new leaves now, like tiny shaving brushes, the brightest green of all, and anyway, she had a message. She was to go to Y Gadlys and ask for green eggs.

Green eggs. She thought it was a joke, but no, her mother's eyes had told her it was true, so clutching the halfcrowns and wrapped up well, though today the wind was warm with a kind of singing in it, she set off, but this time not as far up as the larches. She was to take the track on the right by the stand for the milk churns. The farm called Y Gadlys wasn't far down.

'Would you like to go and look for some yourself?' asked Mrs Ben Davies. 'The hens like to lay in funny places, sometimes. Look, I've got half a dozen here that Ellie can have, but she wants more than that so your mother can take some back, doesn't she? My little black hens are special. There's not many places you can get green eggs.'

On the table in a large brown bowl there were six green eggs, true enough. Of course they weren't that bright green of the new growing leaves of the larches. But greenish, certainly in a pale way, and not the colour of any eggs she'd ever seen before.

And anyway it would be good to explore up there in the barns at Y Gadlys.

She was good at exploring people said, noticing everything, taking it all in, and able to tell you afterwards exactly what she'd seen. Soon she'd found kittens, tortoiseshell they were, and so pretty with the palest blue eyes, playing among the mallow leaves and in and out of the frame of an old mangle. There were bantam cocks there, too, like splashes of fireworks, their colours so bright.

It was up in the hay loft she'd found the hiding places of the little black hens, where they laid their eggs as secrets, and one was warm still. She had a basket to collect them in, a square basket lined with crumpled sheets of the *Flintshire Herald*, and as she was coming down from the loft, backwards, and carefully, on the ladder, Idwal appeared and held the ladder firm for her. She'd seen him before at Ellie's once, when they were hay-making. She didn't think she liked him much but he must be kind because he had a green egg for her and put it in the basket. There was a bit of dirty straw still sticking to it.

'I know where they lay,' he'd said. 'There isn't a place where I can't find them.' And after the dark there in the barn, the feathery feel of cobwebs and the heavy smell of grain, it was a surprise to come out blinking into the sunlight.

After that whenever they went to see Ellie she would go on a message for green eggs. And Idwal would always turn up and put an egg in the bowl.

It was summer now and she was nearly nine, and a big girl everyone said. On this hot day, holiday traffic had held up the bus and made them late, but it didn't matter once they got to where Ellie lived, though of course there was that great walk up the hill first. Up at the top there was a wind blowing like a fragrance and it was cool, though still sunny and the whole hill skiddery with the shadows of clouds. Instead of tea this time there was home-made lemonade to drink and tiny strawberries. Little green tomatoes had been put along the hot kitchen window sill all in a row to ripen. Up at Y Gadlys, though, sheltered as it was in the high elbow of the hill, the air was more still, with a clamminess.

This time Idwal had a secret for her, he told her. And not just the extra egg or two he'd always found. She had got used to him by now.

'Come and sit by here with me,' he said. So she went and sat by him in the hay and he put his big hand under her dress.

'You hold by there,' he said. And she did. And afterwards he had another green egg for her.

Each time she went on the bus to Ellie's there was always the message to Y Gadlys for the green eggs and Idwal would always be there. He would always ask her to sit in the hay with him so she would. She wasn't sure she really liked what he did but he was kind, he must be, finding eggs for her always, and anyway he'd said it was their secret. Could she keep secrets? Solemnly she would nod her head. And he'd always been there, hadn't he? Like the larches, he was part of the place, part of the things that happened there.

She knew he looked forward to their visits. She was special, he told her, and so was he, yes, just like the journey on the bus and the milkshake, the teddy boys on the verandah at The Volunteer, and the bantam cocks and the little black hens. And in spring the lambs in the fields. And sometimes if one of the ewes had died, Ellie would have to rear a pet lamb on the bottle. How she loved to feed it, sitting on the tiled floor among newspapers and old sacking, the feel of its springy gentle wool, so soft, and sometimes it would pee warm and wet down her leg.

Because of being held up in the traffic jam for so long, and you could see it like a many coloured snake writhing along the road down there, like it was miles and miles below them, Idwal had seemed bad tempered when she arrived at Y Gadlys. When she went into the barn to look for eggs, he hadn't waited until she found them, appearing afterwards, as if it was part of a pattern, a right order of doing things. No, he'd been cross, a bit, and a bit rough too, though not hurting her. This time, though, he wanted her to do something different, and because he seemed to want it a lot, she got a bit frightened. He was not so friendly at all, this time, but she did what he asked. And then he went funny and juddery and made noises. And she'd not found any eggs yet.

He did not speak to her afterwards. He covered his face with his hands and his arm then, and wanted to hide himself, all of him, it looked like, in the hay.

She did not go back to the house, to Mrs Ben Davies. She slipped past the kitchen window quickly so they wouldn't see. When she got back to Ellie's she said there were no eggs today, but afterwards they must've found the basket on the floor of the barn, just by the ladder where she'd left it.

A few days later, at home after school, her mother came up the garden with a policeman. She was sitting on the swing Dad had rigged up for her in the door of the shed. And she knew it was something to do with Idwal, just like she knew, even then, that she would say nothing at all.

Later, not long later, a week or two maybe, she found out about an incident. That was the word. Yes. Incident. With a girl. But who could that be, if she'd been special, like Idwal said? Anyway, there'd been complaints. And now the policeman was looking at her very hard, asking her if Idwal had ever said anything to her, or touched her, or asked her to do anything she didn't want to do. She kept saying no to everything. He went away in the end.

She didn't go to Ellie's on the bus with her mother anymore. She didn't want to, she said, though she knew she'd miss the different feel of the place, and the journey, and the larches where God lived. Sometimes she wished she could change her mind and go after all. But then she remembered Ellie's staring. And she could see Mrs Ben Davies going into the washhouse for the basket, the smell of the moist air there, starch and soap and boiled cloths. And she knew she couldn't go back, ever.

And she'd catch her mother giving her the same sideways look she'd seen on the policeman's face that time. A look of wanting to ask more, but not knowing how, a look of not believing.

My Friend of the Earth

I'm glad it's March anyway. Means every time someone comes into the hall and knocks the calendar off the hook we don't have to gaze down at a pair of mating dragonflies in glorious technicolour. So why don't I move the calendar? Tradition, I suppose. I've always had a calendar there. By the phone. But this one? So wide and bulky in a hall so small you can't even swing that proverbial feline? Well, Tom gave it to me, didn't he? It's a long story.

Recycled paper too. *Mais naturellement.* And why should I squirm? What could be more natural than a splendid pair of insects locked obliviously in coital bliss?

Anyway, it's a tree this time. More photogenic. Tasteful. Lit from below and seen through a pink filter. A Jeffrey pine. Never heard of it. The heart of the tree. A Clapham junction of splayed branches, crusted with ice and a snow powdering. On a rocky dome high above Yosemite. Wow! Funny, isn't it, how someone who can get so worked up about natterjack toads and rare wetland flora can be so, well, cavalier about the feelings of a human, female of the species. Me, for God's sake.

Not that you could class him as a cavalier. More of a roundhead, really. I speak figuratively. Hell, what do I care about Tom?

Sally says I'm suffering from the classic case of Other Woman Syndrome. She should know. She's had her share of that particular malady. But it's Easter, isn't it? School's out. And not a moment too soon. The time of rebirth. Yessir. You have been warned.

I'm going to become a born again sybarite. I've bought myself a very expensive Easter egg. I've never done that before. And I've got myself a whole sachet of those gorgeous bath pearls. I was given some for Christmas a while back and I rationed them. Sunday baths only. And only one at a time. But I intend to make up for that parsimonious restraint. I shall indulge myself shamelessly with succession of long Easter soaks. *La Peste* can wait. I know I've been pestering Clarkson to let me teach some VIth Form, but right now I need the bubonic plague like a hole in the head.

I shall go into a cocoon for three whole days. And emerge as my new sparkling self. Who am I trying to kid? I shall keep a diary of my transformation. I haven't done any *serious* writing since I can't remember when. Yes I can. In the run-up to the divorce and just after mother died. But that was therapy. This will be Art.

What a pretentious twat you are, Sylvia.

* * *

Good Friday. When I was a religious maniac I cried all day on Good Friday. I was four. It had been building up for days and worried my mother sick. I started drawing these pictures of tombs and great stones being rolled away and angels. Anorexic types in the style of El Greco. And I went round the house singing 'There is a Green Hill Far Away' in deep lugubrious tones. We used to laugh about it afterwards. Rather nervously. When I was older and wiser and more robust.

'You were such an earnest child.'

What would you think of Tom mother? He's earnest too. Quite unlike David, but you did try to like him, didn't you? For my sake. God it makes me want to start snivelling à la four years old. Only I didn't snivel then, did I? When did the snivelling start?

Less of this. I shall go and run my bath.

I could always have a binge on the sloe gin, couldn't I? Memories. Like the colour of your hair. Why do men get in such a state about going bald? Rare wetland flora and going bald. Is there a connection, I ask myself. Doubt it. Yes, just think, right now, in some exceedingly rare wetland an undistinguished seeming plant, the kind you'd need an electron magnifying glass to see, might hold the secret! Alopecia banished from the face of the earth! Perhaps it was there at my feet among the bog asphodel and the spaghnum moss. And I probably trod on it as Tom scanned the horizon for sight of a marsh harrier. In rapt and concentrated mood . . .

'I don't know why it bothers you,' I said, as the wind whipped his gold and thinning strands, revealing an elegantly bony cranium. 'Anyway,' I said, putting my hand in the clammy pocket of his new waxed cotton coat, his pride and joy, in search of Aniseed Imperials, to which I'm sure I was becoming increasingly addicted, 'Baldness is a sign of virility.'

Oh, the lies we tell . . .

And the day we picked the sloes.

'I love Wales,' he said, with a proprietorial air that annoyed me intensely. Ah, but do you love me, dear Tom? Your little Welsh French mistress, would you believe, your bit on the side? Where do I stand on the sliding scale of significance in the life of a corporate planner? Where does anyone stand? Sometimes I find myself, yes, I admit it, pining for David's total lack of responsibility, his frivolity, his facetiousness. Earnestness can wear you down. The wife, the kids, the company, the mistress. Don't mistresses get fur coats and flowers and diamonds and expensive perfume? Fat chance. Furs are obviously out of the question with a lover as environmentally sound as Tom. The perfume's not on either, the musk thereof and therein being extracted from the gonads of deer or something. Diamonds are South African. Tom, is your liberal conscience for real? I mean, authentic, like we used to say? Are you just another in a long line of pseuds? Flowers, then? Permissible. At a pinch, perhaps. So why do I think myself lucky if I actually get a birthday card?

Because you're a bloody fool, Sylvia. That's Sally's voice. And tone. Worldly wise. Jaded. Pertinent as ever.

Sloes. All over the hedges above the Elwy. High up among the furze and the bracken, the mewing buzzards, and then suddenly in and out of the hedges, a delectation of long tailed tits, tweeting their almost excrutiating high pitched unison cry, their bodies, like pink, white and grey blossoms, those ridiculous tilting tails. And I stand and gulp and grab his arm and see, following them, four or five bullfinches, their breasts like the new deep pink in a child's paintbox, their caps so shiny, so deeply blueblack, with a bloom and a glow on them like the sloes we pick like idiots, packing them tight in a sandwich box, in a carrier bag I have folded in my pocket in case we find an example of that rare wetland specimen. But not up here in the high country. I'm mixing my habitats. See, Tom, what you do to me?

Wherever you are . . .

Guilt is a terrible thing. It corrodes. And this love, and kid myself as I will, it *is* love, can it be wrong? It doesn't feel wrong and that isn't cooking the emotional books, to justify what I want anyway. I do him good. Of that I am convinced. His marriage is all the better for my occasional ministrations. What harm does it do? And anyway I don't feel guilty. Childhood conditioning and all that and I still don't feel guilty. I just wish we could love and be merry for God's sake. I wish it didn't take me hours to reassure him it *is* O.K. That I'm no threat to the rest of his life. That he's safe. But he knows that.

To be trusted implicitly is to be taken for granted. Yes, Sally, I know that too.

I'm wallowing. It's lovely. And if there are better ways of spending a Good Friday morning I don't know what they are. I think the bathroom is the best room in this flat. It's almost the biggest. And there can't be many bathrooms with stained glass in them. I'm glad they retained that section there above the frosted bit. They knew how to build houses in those days. The Edwardian heyday. And all the little servants' rooms under the roof. What architecture doesn't tell us, eh? About social priorities and social assumptions. The mystique of hierarchies. Know something? I've never understood anything at all. Honest. I've never been switched on to reality. To the abiding truths of Realpolitik. I cling to dreams, don't I? Dare I say I cling to ideals? Why not? Still the little flower power child? And does that mean I never grew up?

Did David grow up? He started grown up, didn't he? Knew how to manipulate, to get his own way. Some might call it charm. Perhaps it was. And though no one could say Tom was *charming* he gets his own way too, doesn't he? Devoted wife. (Well, as far as I know. He never says anything to the contrary.) Devoted mistress. How ridiculous. It's hard to imagine any one as *English* as Tom having anything as continental as a mistress. Well, not in the positive, meaningful sense. Is there one? Not in these exquisitely hypocritical islands there isn't. I'm just an executive toy, ain't I?

M'mm. What's new about this though? I've always known the score. *Plus ça change, plus c'est la meme chose.* Too right. And I can always tell by his voice when he phones, and I'm stood there in my poky little box of a hall, contemplating the mating dragonflies. If he's in one of his bright and bullish modes he's just giving me a quick buzz before zooming off to Adelaide or Islamabad. Milan, perhaps. Kyoto. He's showing off, isn't he? But then, just sometime, just ever so occasionally, the voice is different, isn't it? He needs a little reassurance, bless him. A little ego-massage. Which is where I come in. My God, what a wonderfully convenient little creature I am. I'd like a reassurance station too. Where I could pop in for the occasional service, emerge revived, revalidated. Renewed and rejuvenated.

Tough, Sibs. That ain't for the likes of you.

My feet are a *mess*. The reward of thirty-nine years of neglect. Rough skin. Callouses and prehensile toes! Hideous. Never mind. Tom doesn't notice my feet, does he? I'll ask him next time. Next time? Of course, I don't *know* do I? There may never be a next time. Well, if there isn't it'll be a relief, really. Won't it? Dear Tom, I want to ask your advice about my feet. Perhaps my feet are bugging me the way your baldness (incipient) bugs you. What do you recommend for weary feet, ugly and overused? A long soak, says Tom.

Well, after we'd picked all those sloes we had to do something with them, didn't we, children? So it was back to the flat with a bottle of gin and a recipe culled from an ancient cookery book I found in the library. Hell, I don't even like gin. Mother's ruin, yes? Smells like lavender water...

But somehow, weeks later, that first sip. The sloes so long seeped in sugar, in alcohol, and all the condensed effect of that day in the hills. Not even a soupçon of lavender water, and that rich cloudy purple shade. That fire on the tongue.

Why am I a sentimental idiot? No, don't tell me.

This water's going really cold. Damn, I thought I'd left the immersion on. I meant to. Hell, that's the door bell. Who can that be NOW? I'm not answering. They can go away. And if it's important they can come back. I'm on retreat this weekend. I'm in training for when I become a virtual recluse.

* * *

I've always told Tom NOT to land on me out of the blue. And he's never done it before.

Still, there's always a first time, Sally.

You smell nice, he said. I should, I said. Magnolia and lily of the valley bath pearls are very expensive. By the way, I'm glad it's March. I'm sick of looking at those mating dragonflies. Damselflies, he said. Damselflies? I said. Yes, he said. Can't you read? Look. You always were a pedant, I said.

Foxy

Into the cornfields of the Philistines the burning foxes run.
Red gold of the foxes. Red of the flames. Gold of the corn.

I've decided to be me. I know it's living dangerously but I've made up my mind. This is me as I really am. All the highs and all the lows. Intact.

And almost immediately the dreams start. Ordinary daytime things become extraordinary night time marvels. Fine. So far. It's when the extravaganza of sleep slips over into the hours of daylight that the trouble starts. This time though, when the storm comes, I intend to ride it.

I'm an artist. Well, I used to be an artist. But the marvels became terrors and my well meaning husband Giles persuaded me to get expert help. Those were the words he used. Dr Drysdale's expert help was very expensive but his prescriptions worked well. I had no complaints. For peace of mind I was prepared to jettison every creative atom in me. I was thankful for the calm.

And then I met Foxy.

I'm jumping ahead of myself. I must tell you how I came to this outpost in the mountains, this cottage at the end of a narrow valley in north Wales. Our home is called Cae Llwynog. Foxfield in English, but it sounds so ordinary in English. And there's nothing ordinary about this place. Its signature is slate. Look one way and you see nothing but the old quarry workings, the great heaps of slate waste that are almost mountains in themselves. It has its own kind of beauty. Its light and shade, its cloudscapes. I never knew there were so many shades of grey.

I didn't want to come here at all. We had our rural retreat in the Rodings, so easy to get to and from London, so charming too. We still own it, but for the most part Giles rents it out to friends. And friends of friends. But why Wales, I said, nearly seven years ago when he bombarded me with estate agents' brochures and I was merely bemused. I don't think I ever quite worked out why Wales, but that didn't bother me. Giles could afford it. No problem there. And I was so chemically insulated against any form of intrusive reality it could have been anywhere.

And now it's me that loves the place, that hasn't been back to London for years and has no intention of doing so. Giles comes here only occasionally, sometimes with a couple of friends maybe, to do some fishing or just unwind, walking in the hills. They attend to their own requirements, exchange pleasantries with me, nothing more. Everyone back there in my former existence knows Giles and I live separate lives. Perhaps the writers of society diaries would describe us as 'estranged', though they'd be wrong, I think. There's still affection between us.

I haven't told Giles that I've stopped taking my tablets. Not that he'd hit the roof or anything. No, he'd be so very calm, so very reasonable. But Janey, he'd say, don't you think it would be a good idea to O.K. that with Dr Drysdale? No, Giles. You know and I know exactly what Dr Drysdale would say.

But at least this time I've had the admirable and perhaps unusual foresight to cut down slowly on my medication, bit by bit over a period of weeks. Doesn't that go to show that I really mean business? For the first time in years I'm free of my chemical strait jacket.

And I'm feeling fine.

I didn't want to come to Wales it's true, but when I got here (just for long weekends originally till I decided to stay put for good an' all) I decided to learn Welsh. I signed up for one of those intensive courses straightaway. I'm no linguist, believe me, and I got nowhere pretty fast but I did develop a lasting interest in things Welsh, the history, the culture, the legends. I started to read Welsh poetry in translation and, here's the coincidence that so affected me, I came upon that famous poem about the fox by the Parry-Williams or the Williams-Parry fellow, I'm not sure which one, the night before I met Foxy. Well, it was her cub I met initially. He stepped out of the bracken like a little ginger puppy. I nearly fell over him! And he held up his paw as if he wanted me to shake hands with him. You know sometimes things *are* just too cute to be true. Ghastly word cute, I know, but there you are.

The fox cub was there for just a moment and then he seemed to dematerialise back into the bracken. I scanned the bare grassy part of the hillside beyond and sure enough a little while later they emerged, a vixen and three cubs. She stopped and stared at me, at a safe distance, admittedly, but quite without concern.

And that was my first encounter with Foxy.

As I said, I'm an artist. And what I'd hoped would happen happened. Even before I'd stopped the tablets completely the dreams came back. And the ideas, weird ideas sometimes, but I welcomed them all. Not that my first drawings were in the least bit weird.

One of the things you can't help noticing when you come to Wales is the chapels because even the smallest village has at least two of them. I reckon there must've been terrific competition between all the denominations, Baptists and Wesleyans and Calvinists and Congregationalists, all of them striving to build the grandest and the best. Not terribly Christian that, perhaps, and now as the increasingly elderly worshippers decline and die the chapels do the same. More and more you see these often huge places standing empty.

The quintessentially Welsh scene for me is one of an ornately pillared and porticoed chapel set behind railings and wrought iron gates, with, in the background, a hint of mist and fir trees. And then there are those heaps of broken slate glinting in the rain.

Anyway, I started to draw chapels.

I went looking for them. Since I lost my nerve with driving I've taken to the buses in a big way, bizarrely irregular and infrequent as they may be. My chapel studies started as strict architectural drawings. It was as if I had to re-educate my eye. And hand. There'd been a time when I could execute the finest precision drawings with ease. Not now. It was painstakingly hard work. Then, as I grew more confident, I started to sketch more loosely, more in my original style. It was as if I'd had to get back to the mechanics of drawing itself and be sure of that before I could allow myself a freer rein. When Giles came up one weekend after I'd managed to produce quite a fortfolio, I showed him them and was pleased for two reasons, first that he liked them and was glad that I'd revived my former skills, and secondly, and most importantly, that he still had no idea that I'd stopped the medication. There was no real reason why he should have guessed it, since I was perfectly relaxed and contented, but in a way it did indicate how little he understood me. He didn't seem to make the connection. It didn't occur to him that it was strange I should suddenly take up my art again, after years of not even thinking about it.

Cae Llwynog stands on its own at the end of the valley facing the village in an oblique sort of way, looking out on the hugest, grandest chapel you ever saw. Engedi. It was the first chapel I drew, naturally, as it was right on my doorstep. It's been closed for some years now. The few remaining members of the congregation must have rattled about in its vastness, and running costs must have been punitive. I'm not surprised it had to close its doors for the last time and perhaps there's a moral to the story after all. Of the three chapels in the village, this, the biggest and the most grandiose, was the first to close, whilst the smallest and most modest of the three, the plain whitewashed Gosen, is now the only one in use.

Engedi is still an extraordinary monument, its facade being so over the top ornamental it takes some getting used to. Frankly, it's ugly, but so confident in its ugliness as to be almost endearing. I tried to imagine how the original worshippers must have saved and saved to build it, how they must have pondered over the builders' style books of the day before deciding on this dubious combination of Classical pillars and Gothic stained glass in windows incongruously like portholes, except for one quasi rose window dominating all. The whole thing looks sad now. It's emblazoned with FOR SALE signs, and more recently, and more desperately, MAY LET signs as well.

There was never a dull moment at Cae Llwynog. I augmented my chapel sketches with landscapes, moody monochrome things that wouldn't please the tourist but reflected the mountains more truly than sky blue prettiness and sunshine. And I took an increasing interest in the wild life of the area, sketching that too, especially the birds, kestrels and buzzards and the wonderful ravens, nesting high up on the quarry terraces. They're so talkative, constantly chattering amongst themselves. In spring and way into our brief summer, I would listen out for them calling to each other as they soared. And how utterly different were these calls from the harsh croaks we commonly associate with ravens. They were notes of joy, clear as bells.

And all the time I was getting to know Foxy. If a day came and went without my catching at least a glimpse of her I felt quite bereft. I would often go walking up in the hills behind Cae Llwynog, looking for her in a way, I suppose, though at first it hadn't seemed that straightforward. I had only recently acquired this confidence, to go walking on my own. To make me feel really safe though, I always took my grandfather's walking stick along with me, my talisman. It had been kept all these years as a thing of beauty rather than for its practical application, but practical it most certainly was nonetheless and I loved its smooth dark wood, its shape, its fine sense of balance and the band of enscrolled silver on it. I reckoned it brought me luck.

I'd been reading about Australian aboriginal art in one of the journals I'd started subscribing to again. The article was a bit of a hybrid, part artistic critique, part anthropology, but I was fascinated by what it said about the way those truly native people acquire their totems. They don't choose their totems. Their totems chose them.

Surely Foxy had chosen me. I found this whole idea thrilling. I watched her and her little family with growing fascination. I found places where it was easy simply to sit and wait for her to come by. I never tried to hide from her at all. I got to know her body language, what I can only describe as her gestures, her means of communication and believe me, she did communicate. She was not in the least afraid of me and though I never tried to get too close to her and her cubs, I knew that on some level she accepted me. I was not an outsider, not to her. One evening I remember in particular, one of our special September sunsets turning the mountains into a paintbox. I sat there quietly watching Foxy at the edge of the woods. We were both perfectly still, looking sort of sideways at each other. Then as the lightshow moved slowly across the sky the glory of it caught her magnificent white bib and turned it pink, no, more a deep cochineal. She was thin, crumpled and shabby after all that breeding and nurturing, but still with her rich brick colour. Now she was regal. Just sumptuous. And still we watched each other. A mutal frank approval. I felt I accessed her pure intelligence.

I was conscious though, and, not for the first time, that despite the proximity and acceptance of my totem, I could never be a true native. Love of a place is not enough. But even if my ancestry and my language debarred me from really belonging in human terms perhaps I could be redeemed by knowledge. I determined to get to know this land and the creatures of this land in the deepest way possible. It was not going to be just a matter of enjoyable country walks any more. It would involve a proper thorough-going study. I would keep a nature journal. I would observe more rigorously, not simply to enjoy the sights and sounds around me but to understand their interaction, their constant interplay. I would become a true ecologist.

The next time Giles came up he seemed to be rather amused by my acquisition of binoculars and reference books and my new interest in his ordnance survey maps.

I thought he was being patronising and told him so, my earnestness alerting him for the first time that there was, maybe, a difference in me. He began to look at me rather quizzically, keeping his thoughts to himself, though, because Adrian Wallender was staying with us. Giles had shown him my portfolio of chapel studies and he was most enthusiastic. Adrian knows what he's talking about so when he suggested I choose the best of them and write a little history of the chapels, explaining the relevance of each name, for instance, and then send them off to *Resonant Image*, I was all ears. And then he said something about the name Engedi, and how it struck him as strange.

It sounds really Welsh, he said. Don't you think?

And it suddenly struck me too. Yes, it did sound Welsh. It was also unusual. The Horebs and the Salems and the Seions might be commonplace but Engedi was different, special, and, as far as I knew, a one off. I had no idea what it referred to either, so next time I went on the bus to Caernarfon I found myself in the library poring over a Biblical Concordance. Here it was, in the Book of Samuel, the story of David and King Saul, their enmity, and Saul's spies informing him that David was hiding in 'the strongholds of Engedi'. I liked the ring of that, and how, while Saul slept in a mountain cave with all his men about him, David crept up from within the cave's depths and cut off a section of his garment, challenging him later by holding up the piece of cloth to prove how easily he might have killed the sleeping king. Why did this story appeal so much to our valley's quarrymen that they named their proud new chapel after it? I was none the wiser, unless they too thought the word had a Welsh sound to it, and liked, as I did, the idea of 'the strongholds'. For surely these mountains were still a language and a culture's strongholds, even today. I kept repeating the phrase to myself. It had an appropriately bleak, astringent music, did the strongholds of Engedi, with paradoxically, at the same time, a kind of friendliness.

As I sat there in the library the concordance flicked

open to a nearby page and I saw the word 'fox'. Quite casually I looked up the reference in the Book of Judges and read on, intrigued by an astonishing story of lust and violence and horrible revenge. I read with horror and incredulity about Samson gathering together three hundred foxes (now quite how did he do that?) setting fire to their brushes (the implication being that he did this rather as a chainsmoker lights one cigarette from another) and then letting them run loose, the poor panicking things, into the Philistine fields. It was the time of the harvest.

Red gold of the foxes. Red of the flames. Gold of the corn.

I felt that this was my image, that these were my colours. I can't explain it. I was exhilarated, appalled too, but I have to say mostly exhilarated. Something rushed up and out in me, like a log-jam breaking. I knew with growing excitement and conviction that this would become a painting, by far the best, by far the strongest thing I'd ever done. The background of it was there in my mind immediately, familiar as breathing.

Here was my stronghold of Engedi. Here was the view from Cae Llwynog, the row of quarrymen's cottages with the circlet of hills behind, the stark geometrics of the quarry, the heaps of waste and then the chapel itself, handsome and new, a congregation descending its front steps following a sermon, a nineteenth century congregation dressed in all their Sunday finery. A woman is prominent amongst them. She stands a little apart, pointing out across the valley, the foreground of the painting. It was one expanse of wheat. And it's starting to burn, but you guessed that. The painting has a split personality, half painted entirely realistically and with meticulously detailed control, half executed as a Dionysian welter, violently surreal. Half is grey, dark, wet, sombre. You can see the fronds of fern amongst the stones, the individual bricks in the wall. You can smell wet bombazine, wet gaberdine and serge, and the wet leather of hymnbooks. Half is an inferno, of stalks and seedheads, smelling horribly of burning leaf and grain, of singeing hair and fur. And amongst the corn run the glorious flaming foxes, consumed by their own fire, the colours of the sun.

I bought my acrylics, my boards. And I couldn't wait to get home. Did I know then that my latest craziness had begun? I think maybe I did, but if I did, I know, too, that I embraced it.

Leonora Brito

Moonbeam Kisses

The day after the Pope died they put me in an orphanage, which they said was a 'home'. Fair enough. But I fell asleep in the car, and when we got there, all I could hear was this voice saying: 'Welcome to the Home of St Michael and All the Archangels'. Well, I was only nine and although I threw my head back as far as I could, the stone letters over the archway were so tangled up with thorns and leaves and fat white roses that I couldn't make out what they said. Then I saw the nun, kneeling on the path with a trowel in her hands, and I thought I must have died and gone to heaven. Except that I knew, no girl like me would go there.

The nun with the trowel was Sister Mary John. When she stood up, she shook out the black sleeves of her habit like great bat wings and stamped her feet hard so that the loose earth fell over the crazy paving. She wore black wellington boots with the tops turned down like a worky, and she did not smile as she looked at me and said, 'What is it they call you? What?' I told her my name and she grunted. Behind the nun was a stone-rimmed fountain with a statue of Our Lady in the middle of it. Water sprayed up in front of Her outstretched hands, while the first toe of Her right foot flattened the head of a snake completely.

Inside the house, which was tall with windows arched like a church, a small nun with red cheeks smiled and flipped a hand at the bun on top of my head. 'It's Margaret-Rose isn't it? Well, Margaret-Rose, we'll have to get rid of this muff, won't we?' She slapped my hair again and I seemed to see the dust motes whizz around my head like some shameful halo.

'Yes, Sister.'

'Yes,' she clamped her mouth and nodded, 'but it's bath first, then something to eat and then we'll get the pinking shears out!'

By early evening I was tucked up in bed, just like the children in the picture books, and before the curtains were drawn, I lay inside my wide striped sheets and watched the clouds in glory. First they were yellow and pale like gold, then red like lolly ice with the colouring almost sucked out. My head felt small against the pillow and as I watched the rain clouds seep across, I could feel the silver clippers on the back of my neck and hear and nuns crying 'Shorn! Shorn! Shriven!' as the hair came away in clumps. After it was all off they threw it onto the fire where it raised a white wispy smoke that stank.

At St Michael and All the Archangels I was happy for a time. I had a name, Margaret-Rose, and a parentage that put me down in the gold coloured ledgers as 'half-caste'. I knew that this meant me, my arms, my legs, my head, my body. Me. But I did not *understand* until that first evening, when I stood in the darkness of the vestry and dipped my fingers into the tepid waters of the font. Then the words came back into my head and stayed. 'Half-caste'—like the grainy metal surface of the bowl. Greeny-bronze, like metal, half-caste. Later, when groups of children came up to me in the playground and asked if I was from Africa, I shook my head and smiled to reassure them.

Every morning after prayers the nuns gave out milk from a crate, one half-bottle to each child. And we handled the thick cold glass lovingly, walling our eyes on the table-mats in front of us and sucking up the milk through waxed straws, right down to the last trickle. After milk, the nuns asked us questions from the pale blue catechism book.

'Margaret-Rose, who made you? In whose image and likeness were you made?' As soon as Sister repeated the question I became confused. All I could think of was the song playing in Mrs Edwards' house. Sister smiled at me as if she knew the song. And I could hear it playing loudly in my head, the one about 'too many moonbeam kisses, too many sunbeams cooling' and Duggie's voice leaning over me all the time saying, 'I bet you doan know, I bet you doan know . . .' Sister waited and waited for me to speak, then she waved her hand and turned to Claire Tumelty.

Claire Tumelty had eyes like glass alleys and dark, curled hair. She wore pastel coloured skirts with the pleats as rigid as the pleats on a sea-shell; and she did not eat mashed potatoes or drink milk, because she was allergic. Now she sat very still with her hands folded, waiting for Sister to repeat the question. 'Claire, who made you?' And she answered quietly, 'God, God made me.' And Sister said, 'Yes, that's it, that's what I was after,' and turned the page.

I never knew the difference between what I was supposed to know and what I was not supposed to know. Though I sensed that girls like Claire Tumelty always did. She was at St Michael's because her mother was ill, while I had been put there for being 'too knowing'. I remember my foster mother, Mrs Edwards, unwinding the spotted flex from the electric iron and telling the visitor as she plugged it into the wall, that Margaret-Rose was 'knowing, awfully *knowing* for a kiddy as young as she is.' Then she had sighed and said, 'My own were never like it, never.' I left the room and waited on top of the landing until the visitor had gone. When Mrs Edwards called me down I was afraid of what she was going to say, but she only asked me to go to the shops and went on ironing a pile of clothes, including Duggie's vest and things.

That was the evening the Pope died. It was still light when I opened the side-door to put the bottles out. People were burning leaves and rubbish in their gardens and I could smell the smoke as Duggie wheeled his bike in. 'Your old fella's dead then,' he said and laughed. 'Give you something to talk about when you gets to the nuns, woan it?' I had smiled and nodded, though I didn't understand. His eyes glittered like the pieces of coal in the coal-house; and I wondered if it was raining, though I knew that it was not.

The next day I had sat in the back-seat of the car with a

vanity-case on my lap and looked at the sky while Duggie and his girl-friend sat on the bumpy red leather seat of his motor-bike and waited for me to go. The sky was white with thin blue cracks in it like ice floes. I closed my eyes and opened them. Nothing moved. It was as if the world had stopped moving. Duggie's hair was black and shiny with brylcreem, and and girl-friend wore a bri-nylon top with ice-blue stripes. I watched as she tied a red chiffon scarf around her head. I did not know what she was called because she was new, but when the car pulled out and they zoomed in front of us, I saw that they were both wearing dark glasses, and she was holding on, tightly.

Nobody ever told me that roses were a symbol of love, and it wasn't something you could tell just by looking. At St Michael and All the Archangels, the nuns had created a 'Garden of Roses For the Blind'. The roses were all white or cream or the very darkest red, and money and silver paper had been collected to pay for them. On Saturday afternoons most of the children went home, but I was told to go and help Sister in the garden.

At first I thought I had been specially chosen, though I didn't know why. The rich knots of colour embedded in the bushes confused me, while the faint perfume from the single stems gave me a headache. Sister Mary John hardly spoke except to shout 'Mind your feet', or 'Hand me the secateurs—the secateurs!' Yet she showed me how to water all the plants in the green house and how to place the big old fashioned records on the small white plastic record player in the corner. *Where E'er You Walk* and *Now Sleeps the Crimson Petal* were the ones she wanted to hear as she tended the blossoms.

It became my task to keep the records playing. And while they played, I stood quietly in the doorway of the green-house looking out across the garden. From where I was standing I could see the back of Our Lady's head, all grey and crumbly with holes like leprosy; and next to her the black and white figure of Sister Mary John, kneeling on the gravel path, mulching the roses. As I watched, the hiss and crackle of the record mingled with the sounds of the water falling from the fountain and made my heart sad.

'Double blossoms are made in heaven, Margaret-Rose, where are they made?'

'Heaven, Sister.'

'Yes. But you see, the creation of great beauty involves unpleasantness. Always. That is why I seldom wear gloves.' She held out her hands. They were stained and evil smelling where she had smeared and patted the mounds of compost around each stem. I moved my head and she showed her teeth in a smile. 'Don't be afraid of the smell Margaret Rose, the smell won't hurt you. Decayed leaf and vegetable matter, that's all it is.' The amusement in her voice made me feel small; and at the end of the afternoon she remembered it again: 'Oh Margaret-Rose is heaving/ Over leaf-mould smells a-seething, ha! Do you know any poetry?' 'No sister.' 'No!' Her laugh was like a bark and I walked along beside her not knowing what to say. Before we went inside, I asked her quietly if it was a priest who sang on the records, but she said no, it was an Irish tenor.

The time I spent at St Michael's is concertinaed in my mind, with the memories packed up tight or drawn out slowly like a sigh. A week after I arrived, we sat in the main hall and watched the Pope being buried on television. They carried him out on a bier, face up with his hands crossed. His vestments were crimson and gold and he looked like a Punch and Judy man, with the rosy patches on his waxy cheeks and his enormous nose jutting out against the bright blue sky. While we were watching, Claire Tumelty leaned across and asked if she could borrow my vanity case for the week-end. I said no.

Everything is scrunched up in my mind. We said a *De Profundis* for the dead Pope and prayed that perpetual light would shine upon him. Later we were brought in to the hall again to watch the new Pope being elected. The building they showed looked just like the children's clinic across the road from Mrs Edwards' house. I imagined all the cardinals sat inside, waiting for their new father. When the white smoke rose from the chimney and the voice sounded out like a prayer: '*Habemoum Papos*', the nuns all clapped their hands and smiled. Claire Tumelty turned around in her chair to face me and I got ready to say no again. But this time she just looked at me and said, 'How come you never go home on a Saturday, Margaret-Rose? Doesn't anybody want you?'

Afterwards they said I was jealous. Jealous because I hadn't been chosen as a flower-girl. Claire Tumelty was chosen. There were five of them altogether, in long white dresses and pale green satin cloaks. Sister said they looked like angels, with the fresh flowers in their hair and the baskets of petals over their arms. What they had to do was walk in formation—raise a handful of petals to their lips, then turn and scatter them at the feet of the Archbishop walking behind. The ceremony was for the new Pope and in remembrance of the old. The procession should have wound its way through the Garden of Roses for the Blind, but it all took place on the front lawn instead, because of my destructiveness.

I was thinking about the blind as I stood quietly in the garden and tore the roses from their stems. It was nighttime and the sky was dark blue like the blue of a Milk of Magnesia bottle. It shaded out the white and cream and the red of the roses, so that the whole garden looked like an engraving, with everything grey or black. My hands were full of roses. I thought about perpetual light and perpetual darkness as I ripped and tore at the fattest ones. It was the feel of the soft skinned petals falling. They filled my hands and I flung them down. I was sure my eyes looked black. I thought of the black metal box, the meter box, high on the wall in Mrs Edwards' house. Perpetual light and perpetual darkness. When the light went out you had to find your way in the dark. It took ages. Then you reached up and dropped two silver coins in the slot. The light came back on and people slapped your face. Slapped your face and shouted. Shouted.

By the time I came to, I had stripped the garden of over half its roses. Some of the heads lay whole on the gravel path, but a lot of the petals had been dismembered. Sister Mary John slapped me hard across both cheeks and said, 'Lower your brazen face'. My skin felt brazen, hot like metal before it cools, brazen as brass. Then the feeling went, and I stood still as a statue with my head bowed, while two other nuns led her away. I heard them talking about 'a garden lover'; 'a garden lover and a truss of roses'.

The ceremony took place the afternoon before I left. I was put at the back with some of the older girls. They laughed and patted me on the shoulder, and asked me where I was being sent. The sky was white and heavy and it looked as though it was going to rain. After the ceremony, the Archbishop came over to talk to us. Then he blessed us with the sign of the cross and turned to go, but the older girls kept grabbing his hands and shouting 'Father! Father!' laughing up at his face all the while. The nuns tried to move him away gently, but the girls wouldn't let them. They made it into a joke. And the Archbishop went on smiling and trying to claim his hands back. He was dribbling slightly from the corner of his mouth, where he'd had a stroke.

Mama's Baby (Papa's Maybe)

2 summers ago, just after I'd turned fifteen, my mother got ill. One night in our flat on the twelfth floor, she held her face in both hands and said, Leisha, I'm sure I got cancer!

Just so long as you haven't got AIDS I said, and carried on munching my tacos and watching the telly. The tacos were chilli beef'n jalepeno. *Hot. Very hot.* With a glistening oily red sauce that ran down my chin as I spoke.

AIDS? I remember her voice sounding bewildered. What're you talking about, *AIDS?* How the hell could I have *AIDS?* She grabbed at my shoulder. I'm an agoraphobic, I don't hardly go out—

I took my eyes away from the television set and stared at her face. Then I just burst out laughing. I couldn't help myself. I was almost choking. Loretta looked at me as if she didn't know me. J-O-K-E I said, catching my breath and wiping my chin. *Laugh, muvver!*

But she couldn't do that, laugh. Even when I spelt it out for her. Like, AIDS'n agoraphobia—they're mutually exclusive, right? So you haven't got it Lol, have you? She still didn't laugh. She couldn't laugh or be brave or anything like that, my mother Loretta. All she could do was hit me with a slipper and call me stupid.

Orr, Mama! I rubbed at my arm, pretending to be hurt. You can't take a joke, you can't.

No, it's no jokin with you. Loretta got angry as she looked at me. You're gunna bring bad luck on people you are, she said. With your laughin an jokin!

Bring bad luck by laughing? Such *stupidness* I thought, in my own mother. Then I noticed how her body kept shivering as she sat there, squashed into the corner of our red plush settee. And how her hands jerked up and down, even though they were clamped together tight. So tight, that the knuckle bones shone through.

◆

Cancer's a bad thing, Aleisha. My mother shook her head from side to side, and started to cry. A *bad* thing!

Orr Mama, you talks rubbish, you do.

She looked at me through streaming eyes. How do I? she said. How do I talk rubbish?

I shrugged. You just do.

I remembered what she'd said about tampons. Loretta said tampons travelled twice round the body at night, then *lodged*, in your brain. Fact. Even the nuns in school laughed at that one. They said what my mother told me was un-proven, un-scientific and an old wives tale. Chupidness!

Now Loretta was sitting there, crying and talking about cancer. I wished she'd stop. The crying made her dark eyes shine like windows, when the rain falls on them at night. There was light there, but you couldn't see in. Not really. And it made me mad.

Look, why don't you just *stop* crying, I said, adopting a stern voice, a sensible voice. A mother's voice. And get to the Doctor's first thing tomorrow morning and see about yourself?

Loretta looked at me and hiccuped. Then she started crying again. Louder than before. Just phone Joe, she said through her sobs. Phone that boy for me, Leish. I want that boy with me.

Okey-dokey, I took another big mouthful of taco and chewed callously. It was out of my hands now. Now Loretta had asked for Joe. Let Joe deal with it. I stood up. Where's your twenty pence pieces then?

I went off to the call-box with the taste of Mexican take-away still in my mouth. Joe was out with the boys, so I left a message with Donna, who was full of concern. Is it serious? she said.

Serious? Nah. I burped silently into the night as the tacos came back to haunt me. It's not serious, I said. But you know Loretta. My nostrils burned and my eyes filled up with water. You knows my mother, once she gets an idea into her head—

38

Donna laughed brightly and said not to worry. She'd tell Joe as soon as he came in.

Yeah, tell him, I said. Raising my voice as the time ran out and the pips began to bleep. Though it's probably nothing. Something an nothing. Knowin her.

* * *

I was wrong of course. I was wrong about everything under the sun and under the moon. But what did I know? I was fifteen years old that summer, and mostly, I thought like a child.

Like when I was six, nearly seven, I found a big blue ball hidden behind the sliding doors of the wall-unit. I took the ball out, placed it on the floor, and tried to stand on it. Again and again and again. All I wanted to do was to stand on the big blue ball that had misty swirls of white around it. Like the swirls I'd seen on satellite pictures of planet earth.

When I finally managed it—arms outstretched and my feet successfully planted, I felt like a conqueror. A six year old conqueror. *Orr look at this!* I yelled at Joe. *Look Joe, look!* I stayed upright for another dazzling moment. Then the ball rolled under me and I fell backwards, screaming as my elbow hit the floor.

Loretta came out of the bathroom with a face-pack on. She silenced me with a slap. Then she took the comic Joe was reading and threw it in the bin.

Naw, Ma, said Joe. That's my *Desperate Dan* that is.

Too bad, said Loretta. Maybe it'll teach you to look after this kid when I tell you!

Joe laid his head down on the pine-top table, sulking. While I sat on the edge of our scrubby, rust red carpet and hugged my knees. I wasn't worried about Joe getting into trouble on account of me. All I was worried about was the ball. The beautiful blue ball. More than anything in the world I wanted it back.

But Loretta had snatched the ball away from me and was holding it up to the light. Turning it over and over in her hands. As if she was searching for something. But what? What magical thing could she be searching for? I watched the ball turn *blue* under the light-bulb. Then not so blue, then *bluer* again. And it came to me in a sudden flash of wonder—that what my mother was doing was remembering.

But remembering what? Her creamy face was cracking into brown spidery lines, and I got up on my knees, wanting to see more.

Bug-eyes! Joe leaned down from the corner of the table and hissed at me. Fat-head, he said. You boogalooga bug-eyed fat head!

Joe's words put a picture of me inside my head that made me cry. I opened my mouth and wailed until Loretta turned round. Her face had stopped cracking and she looked ordinary.

Joe! she said, how old are you for christ's sake? Tormenting that kid. She's younger than you.

She's a *alien*, said Joe.

Oh don't be so bloody simple! Loretta looked across the room at me. She's your sister

Joe shook his head. She's *not* my sister. He kicked at the leg of the table with his big brown chukka boot. She's my *half* sister, he said.

I remember the words were hardly out of Joe's mouth before Loretta had reached him. Half? she said. Half? She started bouncing the big blue ball upside his head. Who taught you half? I didn't give birth to no halves!

Loretta was mad at Joe. So mad she kept bouncing the ball up-side his head. As if she was determined to knock some sense in. Until Joe (who was twelve, and big for his age) lifted his big clubby arms in front of his face and yelled at her. Get off've me! Fuckin get off've me. Right!

I was scared, then. I thought Joe was in for a hiding. The mother and father of a hiding. But something strange happened, Loretta suddenly upped and threw the ball away from her—just threw it, as if she was the one who was hurt. And as soon as she let the ball go, wonder of wonders, Joe burst into tears and pushed his head against her stomach. Sobbing out loud like a baby, saying, 'S not fair! 's not fair! And asking her over and over again as she cwtched him, How come *my* father never brought *me* no presents, Ma? How come?

Poor Joe! I sat in the middle of our scrubby red carpet, happily hugging the big blue ball to myself. I realised now that I was luckier than Joe. My *half* brother Joe. And quicker than Joe and cleverer than Joe—even though I looked like a *alien*.

Joe was like Loretta. I looked across the room at them, across the scrubby, rust red carpet, that suddenly stretched out vast and empty as the red planet Mars.

You takes after *my* family, Loretta was telling Joe. You takes after *me*.

I felt something like a pang, but it didn't matter. I had the blue ball—which was big enough to stand on, like planet earth. A special ball, bought for me specially, by a strange and wonderful person called *My dad!*

Of course, *my dad* was always more of an idea than anything else. I never saw my real dad when I was a kid. But I clung to the idea of him. In the same way that I clung to image of *my self* at six, triumphantly balancing on the blue, rolling ball. They were secret reminders of who I really was.

I held on to those reminders even more when Loretta was diagnosed as having cancer. They helped me keep my distance. And I needed to keep my distance, because once the hospital people dropped the Big C on her for definite—cancer of the womb, (Intermediary Stage) things got scarey. And while Joe tried to pretend that nothing terrible was happening, or would happen, I knew better. And I made sure I kept my distance from the start.

Like when Loretta had to travel back and fore to the Cancer Clinic for treatment. Joe asked if I'd go with her. Only for the first couple of times, he said. Just to keep her company?

I can't, I said. I've got tests coming up in school.

Tests? Joe looked at me gone off. Tha' Mama's sick, he said. She needs someone with her. I can't go myself cuz I'm in work. His jaw tightened—

I've got a biology test coming up, I said. And maths and history—

Oh leave it Joe, said Loretta. I'm *alright!* She laughed, I'll manage.

Joe umm'd and ah'd a bit, then he gave in. Well, if you're sure, Ma, he said.

Hiding my satisfaction, I picked up my biology textbook, *The Language of The Genes* and began taking seriously detailed notes.

I never did go with Loretta to the Cancer Clinic. Though I could have made time, if I'd wanted. Academic work was easy for me, I enjoyed it. Reading books and doing essays. And tests were almost a doddle. But at home I began making a big thing of it. Hiding behind the high wall of 'my schoolwork' and 'my classes' and my sacrosanct GCSE's, which I wasn't due to sit until the following year anyway.

I also let it be known that I *had* to go out, nights. Most nights, otherwise I'd turn into a complete mental brainiac.

So when Loretta arrived home weak and vomiting from the radium treatment, I'd already be standing in front of the mirror, tonging my hair, or putting on eye make-up. No need to ask where I was going. I going out, to enjoy myself. Even though enjoying myself meant drinking (alco-pops); and smoking, and hanging with the crowd. All the stuff I used to describe as 'too boring and predictable' for anyone with half a brain cell. Now though, it was different. Now I became best mates with a hard faced, loud mouthed girl called Cookie, who Loretta said was 'wild'.

The euphemism made me smile as I rushed around the kitchen filling the kettle and making the tea to go in the flask. I was happy and focussed on what I had to do, knowing that the sooner Loretta was settled, the sooner I'd be out through the door.

Luckily, there was no need to bother with food. Loretta

couldn't swallow any food. Only *Complan*. And *Complan* made her vomit. So she stuck to tea. Weak tea, and sometimes, a couple of mouthfuls of tinned soup. Which I did think was sad, because my mother was a big woman who'd always enjoyed her food.

Now though, she hardly ever went in the kitchen. And it wasn't worth bothering to try and tempt her with anything. But I brought her a cup of tea, and handed it over. Then I put the flask on the little table next to the couch, in easy reach.

Taking a couple of sips of tea, seemed to exhaust her. And she laid her head back on the cushions, tired—but not too tired to speak.

This girl Cookie—she began.

Yeah? By now I'd gone back to the mirror and my mascara.

I don't like the idea of you runnin round with her. Loretta pursed her lips. That girl's trouble, she said. That girl's *hot!*

I was watching her face in the mirror. Her face and my face, side by side. It was eerie seeing us together. Like watching night turn into day or day turn into night. There was no resemblance between us. No real likeness that I could see. And it played on my mind. Who was she, I thought? This big woman lying on a plush red couch, with a green plaid blanket pulled up to her chin?

I crossed over to the couch and looked at her, coldly

What're you talking about *hot*? I said. You're always going on about something.

Loretta sighed.

I just don't want you in no trouble, she said. You nor Joe, come to that.

I'm not gunna *be* in any trouble!

No? Loretta looked up at me and smiled. Well, god be good, she said and crossed herself. Let's hope it'll stay like that.

Listen! I brought my face down close to hers and spoke slowly, deliberately. Cookie's ways, are not my ways, right? My voice grew colder. *Your* ways, are not my ways—

Loretta stared up at my face, trying to understand what I was saying. Then she took a gulp of tea, and her eyes swam with tears.

You little *bitch*, she said. Anybody'd think I was a bad mother to h'yer you speak!

Orr, now come on, Lol.

The rush of energy in her voice had surprised me. And I tried to back away from what I'd started. But Loretta was on a roll.

Did I get rid of you? she said. Did I? No, I kept you. You and Joe. Even though I had no man behind me. And what's my thanks? Her voice grew angrier as she looked at me. *Shit is my thanks!*

I shrugged and tried to move away, but she started off again.

'Course, it'd be different if I was posh, wouldn't it?

Pardon?

They gets rid of their little bye-blows in a minute. Doan they, posh women? When they wanna go to *college* or—have a *career* or something. Loretta looked up at the ceiling and laughed. An no bugger ever says a word. Her voice was disbelieving. Not a bloody word!

For some reason, I found myself laughing along with her. Tickled by the unfairness of it all. Then she closed her eyes again, tired. Look, *get* if you're going, she said. And don't be back yer late.

When I reached the door, I turned to look at her.

D'you want this light left on?

No, out it.

So I flicked the switch, and left her there, in the dark.

It was always a big relief to me when Loretta was taken into hospital.

I was happy then, shepherding her down to the waiting ambulance and handing her in. It felt as though we were celebrities, touched by a black and tragic glamour, as neighbours rushed out of their flats and wished Loretta well, before they waved her off, like royalty.

Back inside, I always walked slowly past the lifts in the entrance hall. Then I'd whizz around the corner and

44

start bounding up the stairs. Two at a time. All the way up to the twelfth floor.

The first few times Loretta went into hospital, I stayed with Joe and Donna in their little two bedroomed. But I didn't feel comfortable there. And when Loretta began to spend longer and longer as an in-patient, I told Joe I preferred to stay where I was, and keep an eye on the flat. Joe stuck out his jaw and said, If that's what you want, Aleisha. I'm not gunna argue.

Which was exactly what I expected him to say. Though I hated him for saying it. After that, it wasn't difficult for me to ease my way out of things, bit by bit.

Whenever I made an appearance at the hospital, I was never on my own. I always came in with a crowd—usually Cookie and her sister, Cherry. Or Cookie and her new man friend, Wayne. I think they all came in with me, because I was only fifteen, and my mother had a terrible illness. It was like something off the telly that appealed to them.

Joe never came in on his own, either. He was always with Donna or one of his mates—usually Deggsie or a caramel coloured boy called Chip-chip, whose teeth were brown and white, like pop-corn.

With so many young people around Loretta's bed, there was never any time for seriousness. All we could do was lark and joke about. Once, Joe and Chip-chip pressed down hard on the foot-pedals of the bed, sending Loretta shooting up in the air. But all she did was laugh and say, Put me down, boys! Put me down, people can see my old blue slippers under there.

It was odd, standing under the bright hospital lights, watching Loretta laughing. And Joe laughing. All of us laughing, as if everything was right with the world. Loretta was queen of the show. She sparkled in company, which was the way she used to be I suppose, when she was young and working in pubs as a barmaid.

One night, Joe and Donna came in carrying a huge bouquet of flowers between them.

Loretta didn't care much for the white chrysanths, but she was chuffed with the card: *Happy memories, luv from*

R *(The Rover)* R was Royston, Joe's father. And he'd been on friendly speaking terms ever since Joe had left school, and met up with him again.

Now he sends me the white *bouquet*, said Loretta fingering the spikey petals. Maybe he wants to marry me?

While the rest of us were laughing, Donna said soppily, Why didn't you marry him then, Lol?

Marry Royston? Prrrfff! Loretta's voice was acid. He was no good, him, Royston. She looked at us. I put his bags outside the door, didn't I? Coming his little ways. I said goodbye, tara, I'm sorry—I needs my space!

Orr, my poor father, said Joe, laughing. I bet you gave that man a hard time! I was in agonies in case anyone mentioned *my* father. But luckily the nurse came round, ringing the hand-bell so we had to go. Good job too, because I would have hated to hear Loretta start in on *my* dad.

As we were leaving, Joe leant over the bed and asked Loretta about her blood count. When she told him it was up a couple of points, he looked relieved. Good work Ma, he said. Good work! And went off happily with Donna.

It maddened me, the way Joe avoided asking the doctors anything. He clung to his ignorance like a baby clinging to a bottle, and I despised him for it. My own behaviour was more rational. Gradually, I dropped off going to the hospital on a regular basis, telling everyone I was studying hard for my 'mocks'. Where we lived, no one understood about 'mocks' and when they were due. Instead, relatives and friends of my mother's admired my determination in carrying on with my schooling. You keep it up girl, they said. You're makin your mother proud!

No-one, not even Joe seemed to realise what I was up to. Though I saw my mother less and less, I always phoned the hospital regularly. How is she? I'd ask dutifully. And I'd end by saying, *please*, give her my love.

But instead of studying, I spent my time lying on the

old red couch where Loretta used to lay, dreaming about my life in the future. *My dad* was somewhere out there, in the future. I knew his name (from my birth-certificate) and that he'd cared enough about me to leave me a gift—the beautiful blue ball. These days, the ball looked like a sunken moon, stuck on top of the wall unit. But I treasured its blue memory, knowing that one day in the starry future, I'd meet my dad, and we'd talk about this gift he'd given me.

Of course, we'd recognise each other instantly—my dad and I, because it was obvious to me, that *his* genes were the dominant genes in my make-up. They were there, encoded in the double helix of my DNA. How else could I account for me?

It was strange how easily—how quickly the time passed, when I was thinking like this. Even when I did put in an appearance at school, I didn't let go of the daydreams. And when scarey night times came around, I'd turn up the mattress on Loretta's bed, and fish out the money she stashed there. Then I'd go off with Cookie and the gang, drinking.

Not that I did much drinking, except for a couple of cans of *Hooch*. Three cans of *Hooch* and I was away. Floating. Doing stupid things. Once, I tried to walk around the side of a mirror in the pub toilets. I couldn't see that the door was only a reflection—and I kept whacking my head on the faecal coloured wall tiles, as I tried to go round it. The side of my head was swollen and smarting when I stopped.

Leisha man you makes me piss! said Cookie, laughing. You really do! It crossed my mind to ask her why I was so funny? And why was she and her sister Cherry, so cool? Both of them wore shiny auburn wigs, like supermodels. And true, they had the clothes. But Cherry was *humungous* in size. And Cookie wasn't much smaller. So how come they were cool?

I opened my mouth to ask—but I couldn't fit the words inside the moment. The moment just went by me.

Pass. So I opened my mouth a bit wider, and started to laugh.

Coming home from a night out, I'd crash down on the old red couch and fall asleep, happy and floating. But in the morning, even before I was properly awake, I'd feel a lump of something miserable pressing on my heart. My eyes would focus slowly, and I'd remember what it was.

* * *

Then one day, I woke up and saw a strip of blue sky through the curtains, and I realised it was spring. For some reason, that made me feel better. So I went and phoned Joe's house, to check on hospital visiting times; and to see who was going in that night.

The minute she picked up the phone and heard my voice, Donna broke down in tears.

Wassamarrer? I said, suddenly fearful.

There was a long, snuffly silence, then Donna managed to speak. She said the consultant had called Joe up to the hospital and explained there was nothing more they could do. Treatment-wise, that was it. Oh, Leisha! I'm so sorry, said Donna sobbing all over again. But there's no hope for her. There's no hope for Loretta!

It sounded like the title of a book, the way she said it: *No Hope for Loretta*. That was my first thought. Then I began to feel empty, as though a stone had dropped inside me. And I needed to sit down, but I couldn't because I was in a call-box.

But how are we gunna tell her? I said, helplessly.

Leave it to Joe, Leish, said Donna, quickly. Joe said he'll deal with it.

Joe will?

Yeah.

So feeling especially childish and helpless, I rang off.

I didn't do any of the things I might have done, like phone the hospital, or actually go in and see my mother. Instead, on a sudden whim, I lifted the telephone directory out of the cubby-hole and began flicking through its pages, idly at first, then with more attention.

It was gone ten when I arrived in school. Calmly, I sat through classes until lunch-time. Then I picked up my bag and my jacket, and left.

Once out of the school-gates I turned right, and onto the high road that ran past the grounds. I walked slowly along, admiring the old fashioned houses, with their soft green lawns and big double-garages. In this area where my school was, all the houses had names instead of numbers. And I said them to myself as I walked along: *Hawthornes, Erw Lon, Primrose View, Tŷ Cerrig, Sovereign Chase*—names that were as anonymous as numbers really, if you thought about it. But I didn't mind. It was such a lovely day, warm and sunny, and I kept looking up at the blue sky, and marvelling at how beautiful a day it was.

When I came to a huge, black and white gabled house, with a big front lawn and a wrought iron-gate marked *Evergreen*, I stopped, and drew in my breath. This was the place where the man who could be my dad lived. *Blyden, D H*. I'd got the name out of the telephone directory that morning. It was almost the same as the one written on my birth certificate under father: *David H Blyden, O/S Student.*

It could be him, I reasoned. It could be my dad, living here in a mock-Tudor house with mullioned windows. Loretta had never had much to say about him, except that he was quiet. But he had his little ways, she'd said, just like they all do. Joe had whispered to me once, that my dad was from Africa. But would an African be living around here? Maybe, I thought, if he had money.

The detached house, like all the surrounding houses was set well back from the road. And on one side there were no neighbours at all. Only a redbrick Observatory and a fenced in tennis court. It was all in keeping, I decided approvingly. Everything was in keeping, so quiet; and cultivated; and tasteful. Then, afraid someone might be watching from the window, I walked up onto the grassy bank, nearer the Observatory, and sat down.

Now I could see the house from the side, facing the sun, with the dark pine tree towering above it. The pine tree was more striking from this side. Its deep green branches seemed to flip out like arrows, right up into the blue sky. As though, I thought admiringly, they were aiming straight into the heart of heaven.

I wondered about my dad, living here. I wondered if he visited the Observatory at night, to study the billions of stars in the universe? If he did, he'd understand just how *little* our lives were, compared to the vast infinity of space. Surely he would? He was the man who had given me the blue ball.

I took a swig from a bottle of water in my bag, and settled back to dream and wonder in the sun.

I imagined my African dad, climbing the steps of the Observatory at dawn; and looking out over the mysteriously empty ball-court. Like a priest in ancient Mexico—except that we were in Wales. But our history class that morning had been about lost civilizations— which was a theory connecting the continent of Africa to the continent of ancient America; and ancient, Celtic Britain. Once, the theory said, we were all connected. That was a big thought. It fed into my mind, and kept my own thoughts turning over and over and over.

It was late in the afternoon when I heard the sound of car wheels crunching over gravel. Someone was parking a car in front of the house. I rose to my feet in a sudden panic. What if this was him? My heart began to pound. *This could be him*, I thought with wonder. This could be *my dad*, arriving home!

Almost against my will, I looked towards the house, and my courage began to seep and drain away from me. Still, I tried to stay calm. It could be my dad, back there, I reasoned. It could be him, it was possible. I knew it was possible, anything was possible—but was it probable?

No, I decided suddenly. No! The sun had gone in behind a cloud, making everything seem colder, less magical. Even the Observatory—looking up at it, I was amazed to see its structure in a new, cold light. It was ordinary and *municipal* looking. Looming like a redbrick kiln against the sky. I looked more closely and saw that its narrow windows or apertures were shuttered over with grey metal grilles. There was a padlock on the entrance door and weeds were sprouting from the brickwork. The place was derelict!

No mysterious ball-court sheltered in its shadow. Just an ordinary tennis court marked out with yellow lines behind the trampled wire-netting. Enough was enough. I swung my bag up over my shoulder, and started walking, fast. I didn't look behind me, not even for a last glimpse of *Evergreen*, with its pine tree standing dark and arrow like against the sky.

* * *

Of course, running away like that allowed me to keep on dreaming. And even before I was half way home, I'd begun to re-shuffle my thoughts. After all, nothing had actually happened, had it? So I could always go there again. Not straightaway, but one day. When I was ready. The choice was mine—

By the time I stepped out of the lift on the twelfth floor, I was actually smiling. It was interesting, exciting even, trying to picture myself, living with my dad in a big gabled house, with a big front lawn, behind a wrought iron gate that said: *Evergreen*.

I was still smiling as I put the key in the lock and gave the door a push. When it swung open, I almost collapsed. Loretta was standing behind the door, wrapped in a red velvet dressing-gown, staring at me.

Ullo stranger, she said, in a croaky voice. Wassamarrer with you, seen a ghost?

Inside the living-room I was surprised to see how everything had been changed round. The old red couch had been pushed to one side and Loretta's bed had been brought in and placed against the far wall. I didn't see Joe at first, hunkered down by the little table, fixing a plug on the lamp. When I did see him, I gave a sigh of relief.

Oh Joe! I said, you're here!

Joe nodded over his shoulder at me, and carried on with what he was doing.

I watched Loretta move slowly across the room. Twice she had to stop and re-tie the belt on her dressing-gown, as it came undone. Then very gingerly and carefully, she lowered herself onto the edge of the bed, and looked at me.

I was terrified.

What're you doing home? I said, in a rush. I didn't know you were coming home—

Loretta began to laugh. She wants to know what I'm doing home, Joe, she said, looking over her shoulder at him. Shall we tell her?

Uh, Ma? said Joe. Too busy screwing a light-bulb into the lamp it seemed, to pay much attention.

But Loretta didn't need his support. Instead, turning back to me she leaned forward, dark eyes shining and whispered, I'm home because I'm *cured*, Aleisha. Ain I Joe? she sang out loudly. Ain I *kewered*, almost?

At that moment, Joe clicked the switch on the table-lamp. Throwing a softly glowing light over everything, including our faces.

There! he said, turning round at last. Sixty watts so it won't burn. That's better, ain it?

* * *

A week later I ran away from home, and two days after that, my mother died. I suppose there was something inevitable about the way those two events were linked. But it didn't seem like that at the time.

That last week, I played along with Joe and Loretta as far as I could. What did I care? And on the Thursday night, when I'd had enough, I went out clubbing with Cookie and Cherry. It wasn't really clubbing. We ended up sitting in the Community Centre, because *I* was broke and Cookie announced suddenly, that she was saving up for a white wedding.

I asked how much it would cost, a white wedding?

Thousand pounds, said Cookie, proudly. The dress alone'll set me back a good couple a hundred.

Wow.

That's because she wants one that flows, said Cherry.

Yeah man! that dress just gorra be *fl-o-w-i-n!* said Cookie, snapping her fingers and laughing.

My mind was troubled, but I laughed along loudly with them. Just to show willing. I even asked about the car. What sort of car would they be having? And Cookie said one with wheels—preferably. And while we were laughing at that, a man came over and asked if he could buy me a drink.

When I said no thanks, he walked away. All nice and polite and everything, but Cookie said I was simple.

He had a fuckin big gold ring on his finger!

Yeah, said Cherry, making her eyes go big. And that twenny pound note he was flashing came off've a roll!

So?

So said Cookie, anybody'd think you won the lottery!

For some reason, I lost my temper and started shouting. I told Cookie if I won the lottery, I'd buy *her* a friggin ticket to Mars. And Joe, I said loudly, I'd buy Joe a ticket to Mars, straight off! Just then a hand tapped me on the shoulder, and I froze. Cookie and Cherry burst out laughing. They knew I thought it was Joe.

But it wasn't Joe, when I turned round. Only his best mate, Chip-chip, wanting to say hello. Naturally he asked how my mother was, and I said fine. She's fine. Then Cookie and Cherry went off to the toilets, and Chip-chip pulled up a stool and sat down. He told me he was working part-time, now. In Mickey D's he said. McDonald's? But really, he said, I'm a *Player*.

A player?

Didn't Joe ever tell you? He smiled, I plays basket-ball!

Oh, yeah, I nodded, basket-ball.

Hey, don't say it like that, said Chip-chip. He pulled a

face at the way I'd said it, making me laugh. *Barsket-bawl!*

I didn't say it like that!

Yes you did, said Chip-chip. Still, it's good to see you smiling. I like to see you smiling, he said. Then he went off and bought us both a couple of soft drinks, to celebrate.

Well kiss to that! said Cookie, coming back to the table half an hour later. Lemonade? That means no major money. She sighed. An having to listen to all that stuff about sport is *so fuckin boring!*

I agreed. But I still thought it was nice for him. Having an interest. His little life is rounded by an *O* I said, picturing the orange basketball spinning through the blue sky. Then I laughed and got up quickly, when the man with the gold ring on his little finger came over, and asked me to dance.

While we were dancing, someone tapped me on the shoulder. I spun round with a smile on my face, thinking it was Chip-chip.

But it was Joe. I shied away from him. But he raised his arm and brought his fist crashing into the middle of my back, again and again. Where's your mother? he said as he punched me. I'll tell you where, he said, punching me. She's in the hospital *dying*, he said, punching me. And where are you? *Out!* he said, punching me. *Enjoyin yourself!*

Joe only allowed Donna to grab hold of his arm when he'd finished. Then the two of them walked out of the Centre, arm in arm.

Most of the sympathy was on my side. People said Joe was taking everything out on me when I wasn't to blame. Neither of us was to blame, they said; and I knew it was true.

But still, I felt guilty

Before going out that night, I'd brought Loretta her cup of tea and her tablets. Eyeing what I had on, she'd asked if I was going out?

Yes, I'm going out, I said coldly. I can go out, can't I? *Now you're on the road to recovery—*

Loretta didn't say anything after that, she just took her

tablets and drank her tea. And I waited until the tablets knocked her out 'dead' as she always said, then I put on my coat flicked off the light; and left her. An hour or two later, Joe had called at the flat, and found her on the floor, haemorrhaging.

I suppose our behaviour that night—mine *and* Joe's, was totally predictable.

A couple of days after the fracas at the Community Centre, I left Cookie's house where I was staying, and went with her and Cherry to the hospital. Joe was sitting in the waiting-room, munching french fries and K.F.C out of a carton. He looked red-eyed and tired. Neither of us spoke. Then Joe pushed the carton of chicken across the table, and told me to take some. I did. Then we both went in and sat with Loretta until she died.

* * *

Inside the cemetery most of the stones are black marble, with fine gold lettering. I like the home-made efforts best. The rough wooden crosses that you see here and there, with 'Mam' or 'Dad' painted on them in thick white letters.

Loretta has a cross like that, though we *are* saving up for a stone. Right now her grave has a blanket covering of long brown pine needles over it. Fallen from the pine tree overhead. There's a row of tall pines all along this side of the cemetery—and I see them differently now, depending on the season.

It's late spring and the sky is blue and the sun is shining. Looking up at a patch of blue, through the pines, I notice the little wooden pine cones, tucked beneath brush after brush of feathery green branches. They're like little brown eggs I say to Chip-chip as I take his arm, and we walk away. Chip-chip says it takes two years for these pine cones to mature and fall, as they're doing now, all around us as we walk. Two years! I think to myself, well, that must be about right.

Hey, Frank Sinatra's dead, says Chip-chip as we reach

the exit gate. He points to a placard across the road. Is he? I say without thinking. Then his arse must be cold. At first, Chip-chip is shocked, then he starts to laugh.

That's your mother talkin that is, he says. That's Loretta!

Yeah, I say looking at him and smiling. I think it is!

GILLIAN CLARKE

A Field of Hay

This is Dafydd's story and he doesn't know the half of it. The field was in his father's keeping. It went with Bethania, Tŷ Capel and the graveyard and they all had to be kept tidy. It had never been ploughed or seeded, but annually renewed itself in successions of orchids, cowslips, buttercups, clover and dog daisies. Occasionally came a glory of some kind—the year of the dandelion, for example, when the field sang sharp gold before the seed-clocks flew in swarms and it was time to cut it down. They killed the hay in July. They scythed, bound and set it up in stooks to bleach in the sun and the salt winds from the Atlantic. Then Elwyn Price would come with his trailer to take the hay. The field was left to settle its roots and grow green again through the dead stalks. Later the scythe was hung in the barn, woodworm in its handle. Then machines cut and baled the hay, and Elwyn Price drove his old Fordson and trailer up the lane, through the gate and into the field to collect it. Elwyn Price always had the hay. Dafydd's father helped and his mother brought tea. They drank it in the sun. There's always sun for hay-making, because a field must wait through the rain to come into its hour at last when a hot, dry spell allows the ritual to begin. So the hay-days of summer are remembered as hot and blue, with a growl of thunder and the first spots of rain as the last load goes home. All the summers of childhood are full of those field-edge teas, wasps and sunburn, thistles and daises bound into stook and bale, into the story of that remembered time. There are photographs in the album to prove it. It had begun long before Dafydd was born.

Dafydd showed Sue the letter the minute it came. She moved their mugs aside, not to spill coffee on it. Letters were rare as home cooking in their flat. The handwriting was half printed, half joined-up, in biro on blue, lined paper. Dafydd was twenty now, and miles from home.

His sisters never wrote. They were almost a generation older. He'd been a late child, son of his parents' middle age. His sisters were strangers with husbands and children of their own. He'd been closer to the sheep-dogs, to the names on the gravestones, to Elwyn Price, than to his sisters as he grew from babyhood and began to adventure into the field. It was not forbidden to him. Its strong gate into the lane was secured with binder twine. The chapel house garden led into the graveyard, and a small gate led into the field. A gap under the hedge, big enough for a sheep-dog or a boy, led from the chapel field into Elwyn Price's farmyard. If the grass was short enough his mother could watch him as she pegged out washing, or through a circle rubbed in the steam of the kitchen window. When the grass was long and the trees densely leafed, she would call now and then, and see the long grass part where her youngest crawled or waded through the depths of the field.

The field was the limit of Dafydd's world. By the time he was three or four years old, when memory began, the field was free to him. Only one thing was now forbidden —Elwyn Price. He must never talk to Elwyn Price. No one in his family would ever again speak of Elwyn Price. One day, old enough to wonder, Dafydd asked his mother why. 'Oh,' she said, twisting dough, her wrap-round apron snowy with flour, 'there was a disagreement. About the hay.' And he was sent to learn his verses for Sunday. The thought of saying his verses on Sunday drove the field from his mind. He felt a lump under his heart like a heavy dinner, and opened the book on the sill of his room, the bright field within view but out of mind, the page brilliant and fearful before him. He repeated the words like a spell, their potency killed by the deadening threat of learning and forgetting and at last coming down to say them in Chapel on Sunday with the other children.

There were two small, dog-eared photographs in the blue envelope Dafydd handed to Sue. She gazed at them. Dafydd, five or six years old, squinted under his fringe into a lost brilliance. His legs were thin between the loose twin loops of his shorts and his wellingtons. Trees blurred behind him. A gate stood open. The pictures were crumpled as if they'd been kept in a wallet, old snaps, the invisible photographer implicit, complicit. The invisible sun, camera and photographer looked into the face of the dazzled boy in the picture and were reflected there. Dafydd remembered earlier pictures, one taken on a beach, where he sat on Elwyn Price's knee beside his mother and Mrs Price on a happy, faded afternoon. He supposed his father must have taken it. Families have drawers full of such pictures which have long forgotten who pulled the trigger. Dafydd knew his photographer. The pictures were the excuse for the letter from Elwyn Price, but not his reason. He'd asked Dafydd's mother for her son's address so that he could send him his pictures. Dafydd had often crawled unseen through the gap in the hedge to talk to his old friend, and from time to time Dafydd's mother greeted Elwyn Price as they passed each other in the lane. She couldn't be doing with men and their old quarrels. But his father never saw him, or spoke to him, or heard his name mentioned. The quarrel over the field of hay had been too bitter. It could never be forgotten. Elwyn Price no longer existed in the world of the chapel verger. The hedge had grown dense and tall against the lane, so that not one window looked at another from the chapel house to the smallholding beyond the field, though their hens sometimes absent-mindedly scratched together in the lane, and Elwyn Price's little cockerel woke Dafydd's father every dawn of his old age, and the graveyard thrushes sang triads promiscuously in border country. The birds and the child moved unharmed through fortifications of bush and briar, over a mined hayfield.

Sue puzzled over the story. She wondered how they managed to erase each other from the small congregation of Bethania, how they avoided seeing the one face, hearing the one voice, forgiving the one trespass. Had Elwyn Price stopped going to Chapel?

Dear Dafydd,
I don't suppose you remember me now but when you were a little boy you were my friend and used to come to see me. I took these photographs of you a long time ago, and I thought you would like to have them. Your mother gave me your address. I hope you are getting on well at College. I am writing to tell you that when I promised I'd buy you a car one day, I put a few hundred pounds into shares for you. They are worth a lot more now. They will be yours next year. I did the same for my boys. I like to watch the papers to see how the shares get on. No one knows about this. It is one of my interests and I promised you I'd put the money by. Do not write back. There is no need. It is a secret.

          Yours sincerely
          Elwyn Price

Dafydd had not seen his old friend for years. Home with his parents for a few weeks that summer, he sat in the long grass and waited, day after day, pretending to read, restless to say thank you. He caught him in the lane. He looked old and thin, as everyone did. Would he be buried in the graveyard? Would his father cut the grass about his enemy's grave, or let him keep his hay?

It was a wink of a moment, a brief thank you, guiltily given like a word with a forbidden lover. Every time Dafydd Price went home he found a way to greet Elwyn Price, who was thinner and older every time.

It was Dafydd's strong, unflinching, unbending father who fell first. Cancer of the gut brought him down, giving his wife the job she'd always needed. She was in charge now, a skilled though untrained nurse, tender and brisk. Dafydd grew close to his father again like when they'd worked the roads together, linesman and boy sharing work and tea and long hot afternoons mending walls, pleaching hedges, scything verges, sharing jokes, stories, father and son so alike in nature and spirit.

In June, on his birthday, Dafydd's money arrived. An unworldly young man, he had not asked, or known how to ask how much there would be. It was ten thousand pounds, enough for a second hand car and a down-payment on a house, or ten acres of good agricultural land. Or an old car, a bit of a house, and a field of hay.

It was Sue who read the documents properly. It was she who noticed the date the shares were bought—the winter before Dafydd was born. 'I don't understand that,' said Dafydd. 'Elwyn Price said he did it when I was small, because I was his friend. Why would he give me money before I was even born?' Dafydd and Sue sipped their coffee in silence. 'You must come home with me to meet Dad. He's very ill, but I'm still just like him.' Sue squeezed his hand and said, 'Yes.'

Dafydd bought a second hand car. He's off home with Sue for the summer, to rev the engine in the lane, to drive his sick father on little outings to the sea, and to cut the hay in the old field.

The Blue Man

Every Friday I'd wheel my bike up the path and lean it against the wooden steps that led to the door. By that time the wetter and colder I was, the happier. My paper-sack was empty, and a saucepan of *cawl* was steaming for me on the ancient Aga. I can still see it. Vivid bits of leek, carrot and turnip bobbing in the bowl, and home-made rolls, all shapes, freckled like the old ladies' hands. One of them would stoop to lift the rolls from the oven with a tea towel, leaning her other hand against her knee to help her straighten up as she turned, smiling, wiping the flour on her pinny. Her sisters would take my coat, give me a hug, sit me down at the table. My mother didn't approve. Weird, she called them. I never got bowls of lamb *cawl* or hugs at home.

It was the last call on my round, last house on the beach road before it fizzled out in a track between sand dunes. Villagers called it the Last House, but at school it was known as Finches' Cottage, a rambling wooden bungalow with a veranda that ran all around it. It boomed like a dull drum, thudded, rattled and breathed. Every footstep echoed on the boards of the long central corridor, filling the rooms with vibrations. The house crackled in frost and creaked in the sun. In winter the wind off the dunes shook and thumped it, sand-blasting the paint from the walls. Outside you could hear the wind whistling in the marram grass, stinging the windows, and a deeper sound like waves breaking in the elms at the edge of the convent lawn. I'd forgotten the elms. Dutch Elm disease must have got them by now. Ghost trees. Does the bell hang in a dead tree? And the nun who used to pull the bell rope morning and evening? Where has she gone? It gives me the creeps to think about things like that.

The autumn after my twelfth birthday, when my mother moved to live in town after the split, I became a boarder. It was a brand-new life. There were only twenty boarders, and to my delight three of us were lodged at Finches' Cottage. It wasn't like being a proper boarder. I had a room of my own, and I was allowed to keep my paper round. My sister went with my mother. The only snag with sleeping at Finches was the walk back from school in the pitch dark after homework. Through the orchard, past the log-shed where the headless man lurked, through the gap in the wall, down steps cut in the rock on which the convent was built, and a scurry down the paved path to the bungalow door. We never thought of torches.

Two Misses Finch and Mrs Price. Three sisters. They had been teachers and had travelled the world. One used to be a missionary till she had her doubts about God. I didn't let the nuns know this, as I wasn't sure about God myself and I didn't want a sermon. On the board floors of their wide wooden house, painted green and cream like a shelter in the park, were rugs in old deep reds and inky blues. There were ivory elephants, which I didn't tell my friends about, carved African heads, and a case of wonderful butterflies. The butterflies on the dunes were like little flags in the wind and you couldn't see them properly. The ones in the case were brilliant as stained glass, so real they might be quivering.

I stopped telling my mother about the Finches. She despised their 'untidiness', what she called 'all those things'. But I was going to have a house like theirs. It was the most beautiful house in the world. I looked at the treasures on Sunday nights by the fire as I ate the treats they saved for me when the younger girls had gone to bed. They had a book of Welsh poetry bound in green leather. It was hand-printed on hand-made paper with rough edges, and on every sheet you could see a pale pattern like a little sickle when you held it against the light. I loved paper. I went in for fancy writing paper, mauve, scented, bevel edged, for long letters to pen-friends full of not quite true descriptions of my life. The initials to the poems in the book were printed in dark red, but best of all were the pictures: engravings of waterfalls, woods, whirlpools and lovers. They made me ache. I had a book that made me feel like that when I was little, but my mother threw it out. I liked the poem book's mysterious language, like a secret code. I knew some of the words, remembered from long-lost Taid who died when I was three. My mother kept her meanest voice for Welsh, probably because of her and Dad not getting on. She had a specially snobbish way of saying 'Welsh!' So one day I intended to learn it.

Elder Miss Finch had collected the books, younger Miss Finch the rugs and butterflies. The Finches were thin and blue-eyed and wore their grey hair in plaits. The elder divided her hair in a single parting from forehead to nape and her plaits began behind her ears, their ends united in a coronet on top of her head. The younger made her plaits into a bun like a pile of rope. They all had red cheeks and wore dark blue fisherman's jumpers for walking through the dunes to the sea. Mrs Price was the youngest, and had white curls. She was plumper than the Finches, untidier, prettier, and jollier. They were all untidy according to my mother, their hair flying like silver grasses, especially when they came up from the beach in the evenings with the sun behind them, flat sandals scuffing the sand, after an afternoon at the summerhouse.

The summerhouse! The bungalow was the last real house on the road, but half a mile on at the very edge of the sea stood a wobbly row of salt-and-sand-blasted huts, leased to fishermen and summer visitors. The Finches had one. They gave me a key and said I could use it to 'study'. I went there once to do my homework. I drank a flask of tea, sat in a whiskery old wicker chair, and waited for something marvellous to happen. I felt scared. Neglected buildings are sad. When they're a bit scruffy they're friendly, then the roof or the windows go and the ghosts move in. I don't want gardens to get all brambly, houses to have broken windows, or people to die. I didn't want Taid to die, or Dad to leave, or my favourite book to be given away. I was scared of the salt-stained glass, the faded cloth at the window, the blistered paint, bladderwrack, rope, driftwood, bird-skulls and oily feathers which cluttered the creepy spaces underneath its legs. It was good when the sun shone, but when shadows came I was glad to scuff home through the soft sand for school tea, jam sandwiches and choir practice.

At Finches Cottage that Sunday night my *cawl* and rolls were ready. The younger girls had gone to bed. I told the sisters I'd done three drawings and my English essay. That pleased them. They opened the cabinet and Mrs Price took out her flints and ammonites and shards of pottery. I've saved this bit up. Mr Price was an archaeologist. They'd lived in Bolivia and he died there. In Bolivia Mrs Price had money, but their government wouldn't let her bring it home. Which would I have chosen? Bolivia, and all the money and treasures you could imagine? Or the Last House? She enjoyed talking about the Bolivian money she would never have. I planned to rescue it for her.

She took out the treasures one by one. I held them, read the little labels and replaced them with exaggerated care. I was allowed to hold anything. Only one object seemed to me too wonderful to touch. This I have saved up till last of all to touch, and last to tell. That special evening Mrs Price lifted the object from its place, held it out to me, and laid it in my hands. A figure five inches tall made of a deep blue mineral. How heavy he was! How cold! She showed me how to turn him slowly away, and how he seemed to smile as the light moved from his gaze to his profile. Again and again I turned him, and he smiled, and slowly back to see his smile diminish. Once someone has smiled at you, you can't forget it. The face has chosen you. Under his tiny plinth was a label marked, in the archaeologist's hand-writing, 'Circa 1100, BC, Egyptian'. He was bald, standing with one foot before the other, his arms folded, 'Lapis Lazuli blue', said Mrs Price. 'A grave god'. Lapis Lazuli! What was he like, her young, dead archaeologist? Black curly hair, I decided, and lapis lazuli eyes. That was when I gave up the idea of being a vet, or a famous novelist. I would be an archaeologist.

My birthday came. I was let off maths homework, the cook made me a cake, and they sang Happy Birthday at tea. I had notepaper with a country scene, a five-year diary, a book about horses, *David Copperfield* by Charles Dickens, and scented soap. And fourteen cards. My mother sent me money. That night there was a little party at Finches. There was a big glass bowl of trifle decorated with tiny silver balls, and a huge chocolate cake on a lacy paper doily on a silver plate. When all the clocks struck eleven, out of tune with each other as usual, I thought it was over and we'd all be sent to bed. The other two girls went to their room, and I was kept back. They wanted a word with me. Footsteps thumped up and down the corridor between the bedroom and the bathroom. Miss Finch with the coiled rope put on Beethoven's 'Moonlight Sonata'. They'd taught me to enjoy things like that. As I told my friends, you've just got to give it a try. Miss Finch with the coronet took out the book of Welsh poems. Mrs Price poured me a very small sherry in a lovely glass that twinkled like diamonds. 'You're a teenager now!' She beamed at me. They'd never given me sherry before. I wouldn't mention this in school. 'We want you to have a present,' she said. I felt hot and excited. I was the favourite. Any minute now a black haired hero with lapis lazuli eyes would arrive. He was already on the road, riding a black horse, or perhaps driving a red sports car.

Mrs Price took the key to the Bolivian archaeologist's case. She opened it. 'I am old,' she said, 'and I know you like these things. Choose something.' I held little pieces of pottery, thinking I would love any of them but for the alluring blue gaze of the little Egyptian grave god. I wished they'd put him away so I could think properly. 'I don't like to say,' I said. 'I don't want to choose something you love too much.' 'Choose!' said Mrs Price. 'It's something we love we want you to have. We can't take them with us when we go.' I felt sick. When they go.

Like everyone else they would go. I concentrated hard again. He was already chosen but I dared not say. Last of all I weighed him in my hand until his coldness was lost and he was blood-warm. I looked at their faces. They were twinkling. One Miss Finch knitted. The other embroidered. Mrs Price looked at me. 'I love him,' I said at last.

'And we love you, my dear,' said Mrs Price, reaching beside her chair. She picked up a wooden box, an inch longer than the blue man, lined with cotton wool that fitted him so exactly that she must have known all the time that I'd choose him.

'To remember us,' she beamed.

I couldn't speak. I wouldn't tell anyone about the blue man, or the tears.

That was years ago. I'm in my first year at University now, doing English, Welsh and Archaeology, and I'm off to the museum to have him valued. At least, I think I am. A couple of times I've been on the brink of asking an expert in antiquities to value him. Then he'd ask, 'Have you something to show me?' 'No', I'd say. 'Just looking.'

I have a terrible confession to make. I've lost the Finches, sort of mislaid them. I left school to do A levels in the college. I wrote to them once. I'd given up scented stationery and had found somewhere you could buy hand made paper. The shop was shut. I would write again when the shop was open. After A levels I went to India, trekking with a friend. I wrote from Delhi. I came back to find my letter returned with 'not known at this address' on it. I was afraid to go back to look for them.

In my head is a derelict house full of the sea wind, and round it the world is falling to ruin. I can hardly breathe. I turn away from the museum desk to check, deep in my bag, for the wooden box. I can't wait to get home, take him out of the box, hold him till he's blood-warm, and be forgiven.

Honey

Only the story knows the when and the where of it. It makes us an offer: enter the myth and it's yours. We can make our lives from the story.

Maybe the story steps into a warm September, the watershed of summer and autumn. Maybe a city, a garden, allotments by a railway line stretched out in the heat, each one a strip of ashy land marked from its neighbour by runner beans, honeysuckle or bindweed, according to the diligence of its gardener, the territory between a railway cutting and a dirt lane. On the other side of the lane is a row of back gardens. It could be anywhere.

The story settles on a strip of black soil rampant with beans and cabbages, tasselled heads of corn, brussel sprouts grown blowzy for want of a sharp frost, squashes resting heavy heads on the earth. Pigeons utter a low bubbling. Bees suck the last of the nectar from sedums and late-flowering ivies. A bicycle leans against a shed.

In the air over the allotments this morning there's a smell of honey and beeswax. In the houses of the keenest gardeners freezers are stuffed with beans, sliced courgettes, rattle-boxes of raspberries. Under the stairs are jars of home-made jam and chutney. Marrows slumber in sheds. Green tomatoes ripen on window sills.

The children are back at school. Tourists have gone. Shoppers and workers have deserted the settlement for the day. Summer rain is done and it's hot, heavy, still. City, town, suburb, village. In September places come into their own again. Gourds ripen. A face looks up from a washing-up bowl and considers disappointment. Summer is over. The red bicycles have gone from the street. There are bleached circles in the grass where paddling pools sagged all summer. They are folded in sheds until spring, the smell of mould locked in. Gourds anticipate candlelit skulls. A train ticks in the cutting. A dog needs a walk.

The story sets out its stall. A swarm of bees, an apple tree, a dog. A train, a box, a tower. A decision, a betrayal, a hoard.

The woman looks up from the washing up bowl, upturns it into the sink and unpeels her pink rubber gloves. The empty gloves lie, palms up and supplicant, on the draining board. Their gesture disturbs her. She turns them over and lays them down together. Now they are praying. She squeezes a worm-cast of hand-cream into the palms of her hands and kneads them slowly. She is a woman at the pit-head kneading her grief in black and white. She's in merciless colour at the broken borders of Eastern Europe. For a moment she belongs to someone else's story.

The hand-cream smells of almond blossom. Her skin drinks it. She looks through the veil of a steamed window. A bubble settles in her hair. Outside, another floats off from the drain and makes for the ether. The dog uncurls from a blanket between the fridge and a cupboard, alerted by the sound of water, the smell of almonds. Signals. He's up and ready, wagging his tail. Dogs are cheerful. They make the best of things. That's why she likes them. She's always had a dog. There was the lurcher, the first border collie, the springer, now another border collie. His beautiful head is up, ears lifted, folded at the tips, his eyes brilliant. She counts her years in dog lives. Hearing the beat of the train, she clears steam from the window with a Jay-cloth. Not that she can see it, hidden deep in the cutting.

At the end of each lot an apple tree leans out over the embankment, laden with ripe fruit seen only by travellers in passing trains. On the inter-city a man in coach C glances up from his book, caught by a sudden thirst for scrumping, a red apple polished on a grubby tee shirt before being bitten, before kissing and temptation. Then he is swept away, out of the woman's story and into his own.

Yellow light over the railway line, the bright, sleeping squashes. For allotment read garden. For squashes read cucumbers. A long ago Sunday school story tells itself to her now. The daughter of Zion is left as a cottage in a vineyard, as a lodge in a garden of cucumbers, as a besieged city. Blodeuwedd steps from the dewy grasses of the morning, heartless as the flowers she is made from. Eve polishes a Cox's orange pippin, and offers it. Those were the first stories, mixed with secrets whispered by adults behind their hands, mouthing, not in front of the child. Her mother and her mother's friend dancing to records on a radiogram with lonely Canadian airmen from the camp. Parcels of tinned pineapple, spam, chewing gum and nylons from America. Ena. That was her name, her mother's friend whose husband never came back. He was an airman. Lost. A word from fairy stories and *The Sunday Mirror*.

Once, when she was four, before her sister was born, her mother and Ena lolled in the garden gossiping and giggling. She listened from the sand-pit. The women mouthed secrets to each other, rolling their eyes. Then, What a lovely castle! they said aloud in sing-song voices. Her mother lay back and clasped her belly. She sent Ena a silent message, There was another one!, and glanced at the listening child. Too late. She had read but not understood the women's message, and she kept it in her heart for later. Later, when she was older and understood more, she wondered. A miscarriage! A lost, longed-for brother? Was it before the baby who would be her sister? Her own twin? She strained to remember that first place. Had she swum alone in that hot sea, or with another? Surely if you stare long enough into memory you can make yourself remember. She grieved for that other lost self, her own reflection fallen back into the waters of the mountain lake as she stepped ashore out of her element, leaving behind her sisterly shadow. In the story she chose earth, flesh and blood, in place of watery reflections. She never asked her mother, though the notion never left her.

They met at university. They were made for each other, her mother said. Made. Like Blodeuwedd for Lleu. Only instead of oak-flowers and broom and meadowsweet it was background, upbringing, expectation, sugar and spice and all things nice. Lleu, off hunting, fighting the king's war, or away at the office. He had a good job in the bank, he was well spoken, three years older, three inches taller than her. That was how it should be. Slugs and snails and puppy dogs tails. She saved herself for him as she'd saved the electric kettle and the toaster and the towel set and the hostess trolley. That's what you did then. All untouched before the wedding, safe in her mother's house.

Yellow light over the garden of cucumbers. She inhales it into the twin trees of her lungs until the furthest tips are lit. Hope is hot gold. It sweeps away a prevailing mood of disappointment. The dog breathes it, or smells it. Who knows how a dog understands the universe, or how much more we could know if they could teach us the knack?

An apple, a dog lead, a polythene bag. You never know. She walks towards the railway line, towards the strips of cultivated or neglected land, small tracts that were gardens, countryside, wilderness, Eden. A mountain track. Calling at a farm to ask for a glass of water in the hope of something better—orange squash, a fairy cake. A cliff path winding down, slippery and treacherous, to a secret beach. A kissing gate. Touch and go. Holding hands with someone. A fizz of damp skin and salty breath. Who? A bike ride with a picnic in a saddlebag, freewheeling a hot tar road. Lying in the allotments stealing strawberries, sunburnt and dizzy, his nose freckled, his arms brown in a blue tee shirt. A cool church where she presses a primrose on page 248 of the bible on the lectern. She can't for the life of her remember numbers now, not new ones, but she remembers old ones, the page of that bible, the reg. of the first family car, their first phone number.

The story chooses threes and sevens. Three caskets, three wishes. That means there'll be a third, she would say after hearing of two deaths, or dropping a cup and then tripping over the Hoover. All day she'd wait for it, the third thing. The story brings a river to cross, a monster to slay, a giant to overcome. Seven was for dwarfs, virtues, deadly sins.

Some days are numberless. A day mitching school with a friend, eating blackberries, peeing behind the nettles, her friend on the look-out. Hiding in long grass, breathless with secrets about boys and God knows what. Perhaps with the story they were about to enter. She remembers waking one day when she was about three and discovering consciousness. Me-ness. Years later she still puzzles until she is dizzy with the mystery. Who am I? Who are you? Time was another one, nearly as frightening as Who Made God. What is time? Is it a road you go along once and never again? Or is it there all at once? It makes you shiver to think about it. There is a big shed with birds, sudden wings and screaming, and two falling into hay. Sunstroke. Migraine. A swarm of bees humming louder and louder to a great crescendo of wavering but unbroken music. And joy.

She walks onto the bridge and stops to looks down, feeling a wave of vertigo. Heat pools in the cutting and rises with smells of ashy soil, nettles, valerian and cat-piss. If a train comes now what will she do? She used to throw apple cores and wave to the driver. Once she longed to jump, not in despair, but because vertigo ran through her like voltage and jerked her heart. She saw the void, heard them tell her story, watched her funeral. She shouted into the cry of the train. Today she would be six, sixteen, sixty, all the ages she had been and would yet be. The story contains a train. When the train has moaned past it will leave the cutting empty of all but its echo and the stilling pool of heat.

But no train comes. She returns to the dirt track, and walks on. Her dog bounds ahead, stopping to sniff and mark each gate. He disappears, then runs back to the bend in the path where he can see her. He waits a moment, ears lifted, head on one side, returns to exchange their sign of belonging and takes off again along the sandy path past back gardens to the right, and every kind of makeshift gate and barrier to the allotments on the left. The dog enters the story.

Someone pegs out washing. A woman gathers beans in a trug. An old man tends cabbages, carrots and prize leeks. They murmur and nod. She walks on with gifts, a handful of beans and some earthy carrots in her polythene bag. She puts her apple in her pocket, and stows the loaded bag under the hedge to collect on her return.

On she goes, her hands empty, wearing the dog's lead like a necklace. On past strips returned to wilderness, tumble-down sheds, leaning gates, sagging fences, weedy jungles. She is heartened by the wild gardens, though the neat ones are more admirable. One puts in a word for nature, the other for the likes of her. She loves the way nature fills every cranny, how it can crack tarmac and seed the desert as soon as we've done our worst. At the end of the track, where the land runs out of habitation, is a red brick tower, then small scraped fields with rusty sheds where ponies starve. A disused, three storey tower, a garden of fruit trees and bee-hives.

A tower with a white face at a high window. A rope of yellow hair. A horseman. A railway line where two steal strawberries and peas from silent allotments, where a hermit lives on windfalls and wild honey. Where her child-days are played out over the fields, and she sucks the ends of pulled grasses, eases honeysuckle, clover and fuschia from the calyx for its one droplet of nectar. She is an anchorite in the desert. She is Branwen with her starling, banished from her estranged husband, King of Ireland. Once upon a time children knew, as stories did, the difference between the nourishing and the poisonous, blackberries from nightshade, bread-and-cheese from monkshood, a sweet grass from a laburnum pod. Once, for a dare, she sucks the flesh of the deadly yew-berry, knowing that one seed accidentally swallowed means certain death.

She and the dog have walked a long way, miles along the track. Heat rises and the railway lines swim in a dazzle of convergence that wavers like migraine. Someone is moving in the last allotment, half-hidden by bean tunnels, apple trees and the weedy edges of no-man's-land. Someone is tending bees. He will greet her as she passes. He will remember the captured swarm last time she walked this far. There are four hives here, in the last allotment. Inside, she knows, each one is a cathedral, its wax vaults and draperies spun by thousands of workers. Inside each one the queen considers the swarm. To fill the larder before winter is a matter of life or death. Crucial, too, the strength and balance of its population, the interdependency of its society, the hierarchy of its court. In each hive is orderliness, beauty, a restless surge of wings. As her mother would have said, like a little palace, so clean you could eat your dinner off the floor. A swarm of bees in June is worth a silver spoon. But a swarm in July.

That July day weeks back something had moved in the queen, who is the mind and heart of the body called swarm. Instinct surged through her. To fly, up sticks and go, to leave her palace of wax where the infant bees were raised, where she feasted on nothing but royal jelly, where, once his sperm was taken, every male was driven out and stung to death. Despite all, she would go, taking 60,000 female worker bees with her, with no sure place to rest before the dark. The swarm hummed in the apple tree. The man turned, his hand out in a gesture that said, keep back. She clipped on the dog's lead and hooked the loop over a gate post. Sit, she said, Stay. Quiet. And she entered the allotment. The dog lay, ears up, eyes on her every movement.

No word spoken. The man looked at her quickly, a question in his eyes. His eyes were like bees. She'd noticed this before. Her eyes said, I know what to do. The tree weighed its dark fruit. The hot core of bees, the loose aura of dancers. A whirling dervish. His thin hands, his arms brown below the rolled-up sleeves of a blue denim shirt. He held the box under the swarm, and she, at his glance, struck the branch a sharp blow. The swarm fell into the box. She imagined it surprised into falling, like a limpet prised from a rock too quickly to tighten its grip. The man shut the lid of the box. Leftover bees attended the branch as if they still belonged to something. They would linger lovesick and doomed about the branch where their queen left her scent, but their only need now was to grieve, and to die.

As the man carried the box away she stood still for a moment as if held by something, then felt it slip from her. He had gone, into the tower. It looked cool and dark in there. She unleashed the dog and they went their way. The last swarm was years ago. Another life, another self, inside her.

She is sixteen. A swarm hangs humming in a tree. Two hold their breath, whispering. He lays his brown hand, stained with stolen fruit, on her arm, her brown skin reddened from another day of sun. The bees hold on, a singing bell entranced by the queen-smell.

A swarm of bees in May is worth a load of hay, the old man never tired of telling them. After that, diminishing returns. There'd be an old queen at the heart of this dark humming. Boxed, moved into a hive, fed with sugar to keep it going through the winter, and no honey till next year. They don't think twice about saving the swarm. To save the bees is to save summer. The swarm is an animal. They love animals. It's their bond.

They take the key from its impression in the earth under the stone, unlock the shed, take the box from its corner. Outside the swarm hangs, accumulating more and more bees, dark, loud and growing inside an aura of workers flying in to join it. They daren't wait till they're all attached. He will hold the box firmly. She will give the branch a sharp knock. The swarm will drop into the box, the lid click home, and they will retreat without a sting, proud of their deftness, happy the swarm is safe and on its way to a new hive. The lost ones will make them sad. For days it will hurt to see the lost bees dance about the empty branch, fewer and fewer until not one is left.

It doesn't happen like that. Somewhere deep in the

core of the swarm the old queen has a thought. The thought runs like mysterious electricity, a high pitched song in the wires of the swarm. Uncertain, restless, something like: not yet, not here. Bees loosen and the swarm collapses, unforms, lifts, a singing cloud. He sets the box down and they step back into the doorway. The swarm swallows the brilliance. A second before it happens he takes her arms and straightens them in front of her body, he clasps her, ropes her to him, presses her face against his blue shirt crushing her body to his body as if he has stolen her. The queen settles in her hair. The swarm is a muffled psalm because her ears, eyes, mouth, nose are pressed into the sweat and prickle of him and she cannot move. He is hot, fierce, a twin in the womb. She's done for. His heart beats in her mouth. Everything will be less than this, the terror, intimacy, rising sound, the organ's toccata and fugue. She's inside the instrument, under the drum of his heart. Locked in. Punished. Ecstatic. Even muffled, it's deafening, a low humming with a sharp wire of high notes among the basso profundo. She doesn't struggle. That's the odd thing. Fear turns docile. The fight goes out of her. Every nerve-tree wired, every branch blossoming. And both of them done for.

Once, swimming in a wild sea, a huge wave mounted and fell upon her and she knew herself drowned in crushing splinters of water, sinking through depths of shining commotion. Then she lay on the sand again, alive. The sea had let her go.

He lets her go. Thanks, she says, weeping. The queen decides on the tree after all. She is dizzy. He picks stings from her hair, then his arms. It seems like nothing after drowning. So quiet now her ears hum. They stroke each other's skin with dock leaves. They wipe tears. They kiss with swollen mouths. He saved her, like in dreams. They caught the swarm alone. It sings in its box in the shed. They lie in the cold grass as dusk draws over the allotments and the railway line. Maybe tomorrow the old man will let them help take honey from the hives. They will spin and jar the honey, licking their fingers until they are again drunk on sweetness and dizzy from standing so long over the steam of the separator box watching wax rise and the overflow of hot honey run from the spout into the steel kettle. When the golden rope has filled another jar for sealing they will lick the droplet left after closing the tap of the drum. They will break off pieces of floating honeycomb and feed each other, crushing honeycomb between tongue and palate till the sweetness runs, laughing till the old man tells them to stop, stop. There'll still be a fragment of wax on their tongues as they walk home in the dark, dawdling by the railway line, an owl somewhere, and a tree with the moon in it. Blodeuwedd sucks honey, wondering at the owl's note of sorrow.

That was then. Now it is September by the railway line. It's another century.

Hello.

Oh. It's you. I've made tea. Would you like a cup?

The interior of the tower is dark and cool. One small dark space, not a room, really, or a shed, but an anchorite's cell. It serves as a garden shed, with a sink, a stove, a bench, a small window, a spiral flight of iron stairs.

What is it? she asks. Is it yours?

Belonged to the railway, he replies. I bought it. The planners won't let me convert it, but I like it as it is. I sort of camp out here. Don't tell! As far as they're concerned it's a garden shed. My wife has the house.

What's up those stairs?

Come and look. Bring your tea.

Up winding steps to a round room furnished with a tattered leather arm chair, a camp bed, a card table with a blue oilcloth, a wooden chair. She steadies herself.

I'm sorry, she says. A headache from the sun.

I'll leave you here. Have a rest. I'll be working outside. Don't worry.

She feels tipsy. She should have seen this coming. Every sound, every movement hammers the interior of her left temple. Her body is drawn down into the cool leather of the chair. She is losing her battle with gravity. She must sit still inside her head. The story leaves her asleep in the tower. The daughter of Zion is left as a cottage in a vineyard, as a lodge in a garden of cucumbers.

She wakes, hours later. For a while she doesn't even open her eyes. Something damp covers her forehead and eyes. A step on the stairs.

You're awake. How are you? It's evening. Will you get into trouble?

There's no one at home. I'm fine now. I'm so sorry.

It's OK. How do you like my poultice? You were asleep. It's good for sunstroke.

She lifts a wad of leaves, darkened now, from her forehead, and sits up straight.

Dock leaves. Come down when you want to.

She doesn't feel afraid in the stranger's tower, or shy, or embarrassed that he has seen her ill, that he placed a folded poultice of cool leaves on her forehead as she slept. Like somewhere she has been before.

A brown earthenware pot of tea, a plate of bread and butter.

That's perfect. It's what I always have after a migraine. I feel brand new now. I always do.

The honey drums are upside down on the draining board, the separator tilted over the sink. The shelves are full of jars of honey. There's a stainless steel separating pot on the stove, melting the residue of honey and wax. Later, when it's cool, the honey will be poured through the overflow pipe from under the cooled crust of wax.

It's nice here. I like towers.

I've wanted to live in one.

What's on the top floor?

Blodeuwedd lives there. She's a barn owl.

Yes. Fancy you knowing the story.

I keep her company. We're both sinners. Me, her and the bees. A bee settled on Plato's lip when he was a baby, bringing him the gift of honeyed words.

I thought that was St Ambrose.

According to Mahomet bees are souls.

God! I must go.
I'll see you home.
I'm not sure. Well, just to the railway bridge.

The moon is in a tree. The barn owl sweeps down over the allotments. A train cries into view, for a moment dowsing the track. It brings the workers home from the city to the suburb, to the village. The bee-keeper leaves her at the bridge, and watches her and her dog out of sight.

At her back gate she stops suddenly, caught by the clarity of an after-migraine moment, the ice-clean clearness the visionaries must have known. Then, for the first time for years, a sheet of searing joy. It sweeps away a prevailing mood of disappointment. It blazes. It takes her breath away. Flames lick her ribs. Sparks needle her toes. The dog observes it, or breathes it, or hears it.

Then, as she turns to the house, a moment of dread.

Where you made your summer's honey, there make your winter quarters, the cruel king said to the queen bee as he turned her away when she and her swarm, lost in a storm, called at his door begging shelter.

She tips the washing up bowl, and squeezes a curl of hand-cream into her palm, kneads her hands and considers whether disappointment, rather than loss, is the heavier burden. Today her heart is not rescued by a sheet of yellow light. It is a stone. Then someone steps into her garden from the ash-track. She swirls a clearing in the steam. He is standing outside the window, raising a jar of amber into the morning light. Honey. He mouths. The dog rushes barking to the window. She opens the back door. She does not like to assume the honey is for her, or that it is not.

Oh?

He hands it to her.

Thank you for helping. I meant to give it you last night.

Oh! It's all right. Would you like?

Well.

He does not step away.

Come in. Would you like coffee?
No. No. Better not.
The dog is welcoming now, curling and licking the almost stranger.
What a lot of bees.
Not another swarm I hope.
No. Too late.
Your bees come here. They like the sedum.
Well, it's your nectar then. Yours already really.
She laughs and looks away, as if reading a script. The dog is an initial on a medieval manuscript. A train moans by.
Again. Any time. Help me with the bees.
Yes. I'd like that.
Tomorrow? I'm taking more honey tomorrow.
Yes. Yes.
And he's gone. Thin, running on the track. The story tells itself in her head. A swarm of bees, an apple tree, a dog. A train, a box, a ruined tower. A decision, a betrayal, a gold-hoard.

Jo Hughes

Too Perfect

The man and the woman were standing side by side at the marina studying the new housing development on the other side of the water. He had been expressing surprise, tinged with disgust, at the sight of the red-brick buildings with their gabled windows and arches and as he put it 'post modern gee-gaws'. While she, having no knowledge of what had stood there before and no great opinion on architecture, said nothing.

Then into the silence that hovered between them he suddenly offered 'Do you mind?' and before he had finished asking, took her hand in his. In reply she gave a squeeze of assent, noting as she did how large and warm and smooth his hand was.

To a passerby it would have looked like nothing out of the ordinary. He or she, on seeing this man and woman by the water's edge, would assume that this hand holding was a commonplace event for them. But it wasn't. This was the first, the only time of any real physical contact between them.

Later, still awkwardly holding hands, each now afraid that letting go might signal some end to that which had not yet even begun, they made their way to the old Town Hall; once the home of commerce and council and now a centre for literature. This was the purpose of their trip, the reason why at seven that morning, she had stood at the window of her bedsit in Cambrian Street, Aberystwyth, waiting for the tin soldier red of his Citroen to emerge around the corner.

Each had expressed an interest in visiting the centre and had behaved as if they were the only two people in the world with such a desire. That was why, uncharacteristically, he hadn't suggested the trip to the other members of his tutorial group. It was also the reason why she had omitted to tell any of her friends. Why she had agreed to wake Ginny that morning at ten o'clock, despite the fact that she and Dr Terrence Stevenson would be, probably, enjoying coffee and toast together in Swansea by then.

Terry, as he was known to colleagues and students alike, was a large man, over six feet, with large bones and large appetites, which now, as he neared fifty, expressed itself in its frame. He had once been lithe and muscular, but his body had thickened with age. He blamed too many years at a desk, the expansion of his mind at the expense of an expanding behind. But he dressed well enough, choosing dark tailored jackets and corduroy or chino slacks, as well as the odd devilish tie which was about as subversive as he got. In colder weather, as on this grey October day, he wore his favourite black Abercrombie overcoat. The coat hung well from the shoulders and had the effect of tapering his body, disguising its imperfections with a veneer of powerful authority and masculinity.

Claire thought he looked like one of the Kray twins in this coat of his and to her that signalled a sort of dangerous sexuality. She could not help but imagine herself engulfed in that coat, held willing captive in its soft folds.

Next to him, she looked tiny, even less than her five feet and a half inch. Claire had very long hair, grown in excess to compensate, perhaps, for her lack of height. It hung down, straight and sleek to her hips, and a great deal of her time was taken up with this hair: washing, combing and plaiting it before she went to bed each night. Most of the time she wore it loose and her gestures, the movement of her head, body and hands were all done in such a way as to accommodate this river of hair. When eating, for example, she would hold the fork in one hand while with the other she held her hair away from the plate. She was very proud of her hair and if asked which part of herself she liked the most, the reply would always be her hair. Her last boyfriend, whom she had met at the fresher's dance at college and dated for two years, had loved her hair; had sometimes spread it over her naked body, Lady Godiva-style when they made love; had once even made the pretence of tying himself to her by it.

Claire's body was like a boy's: flat-chested and slim-hipped. And today she was dressed like a boy too, with jeans and heavy black lace-up boots and a white shirt and a man's tweed jacket two sizes too big. Through both her right eyebrow and right nostril she wore tiny silver rings and her eyes and lips were exaggerated with make up in shades of reddish brown. She seldom smiled, but when she did her entire face was transformed into, if not quite something beautiful, then something very like it.

They had trudged through an exhibition of artefacts relating to the town's one famous poet: the scribbled postcards, the crumpled snapshots, the yellowing newspaper clippings, all framed and glass-cased for posterity like the relics of some dead saint. Terry had begun by clucking and tutting yet more disapproval of the venture, disapproval he'd been nurturing and planning since he first heard of it, but with Claire by his side he found himself softening, growing acclimatized to her open-minded acceptance of all such endeavours.

They spoke in whispers, though the place was almost entirely deserted, this being after all a grey Monday in October, and around the back, beneath some etchings by Peter Blake they kissed their first kiss. It did not feel like the world's best kiss for either of them, but it did well enough as an awkward, uncertain snatched preliminary to better things. Afterwards Claire had wanted to wipe her mouth with the back of her hand, not from disgust, but just because the kiss was a little wet. His mouth had swallowed hers, had not measured out the size of her lips yet.

After the kiss they each felt like a conspirator in some deadly plot; what they would create that day felt as if it might be as deadly as Guy Fawkes' gunpowder, as world changing as any revolution.

The second kiss came as they sat in a deserted pub. The barman, a student, they decided, was propped against the far end of the counter, his head bent over a book. They took turns to guess what the book might be. Terry said it was a handbook about computing, and she thought it was the script of something like Reservoir Dogs.

The clock above the bar, a faux-nautical affair, hung with nets and cork floats and plastic lobster and crab, read twelve-fifteen. They had the afternoon and the early evening to spend together. He was thinking about the Gower coast, a cliff walk, the lonely cry of the curlew and the sea, a grey squall bubbling under the wind. She was thinking about a hotel room, the luggageless afternoon ascent in the lift to the en suite room and the champagne, herself languishing on the sheets, feeling intolerably beautiful under his grateful gaze.

After that second kiss, which was prolonged, they wrenched themselves away and began to speak in a strange language of unfinished sentences and hesitant murmurings.

'Oh.'
'Gosh.'
'You know we . . .'
'I never . . .'
'Oh my . . .'
'We shouldn't . . .'
'I never thought . . .'
'Nor me . . .'
'I mean, I always thought that maybe . . .'
'Me, too . . .'

Then they kissed again and the barman, who wasn't a student, raising his eyes briefly from his novel by Gorky, watched them with mild interest and thought they made an odd pair.

The odd pair finished their drinks; cloudy pints of real ale. She stubbed out her cigarette and they made their way towards the exit, his arm thrown protectively around her shoulders, while his broad back wore her tiny arm, its fingers clutching the cloth, like a curious half-belt.

The sky looked, by now, greyer and darker than before. To the west, a blue-black curtain advanced promising heavy rain and a wind blew up from the east sending her hair on a frantic aerial dance. They ran across the empty square as raindrops as big as shillings began marking the paving stones with dark circles.

Then she half-stumbled and he caught her, and in catching her, gathered her to him and they kissed a fourth time, this the best, with the rain splashing their heads and water pouring down their faces.

When they had done with this, this their unspoken moment of willingness and promise and willfulness, their pact to indulge in what they knew was an unwise thing, he quickly kissed the tip of her nose and then, hand in hand, they began to run again.

Under the covered walkway, they slowed down and shaking the worst of the rain from their hair and clothes, they barely noticed a man standing close by. He was busy putting away a tripod and Terry muttered, 'Afternoon,' and the man, grinning broadly replied, 'Thanks'.

Naturally neither of them made much of this, assuming it to be yet another curious aspect of Welshness. A further example of the strange smiling politeness, the thanking of bus drivers and so on, the chatting to strangers which each of them had at first perceived as alien, but now, despite their breeding, accepted and in part, adopted.

Later that afternoon, in his car near a field in the north of Gower, with the day as dark as ever they almost made love. The next day, back in Aberystwyth, they did make love.

She had rung him from the pay phone in the hall of her house when she was certain that all the other students had gone out. His wife had answered the phone and she'd given her the prearranged message which was that she'd 'found the journal with the Lawrence article he'd wanted.'

What happened that Wednesday was perhaps rather sad, though not necessarily inevitable. It became clear to both of them that they each sought a fugitive moment, that there could be no more than this; the furtive opening of the front door, the climbing of the stairs, the single bed dishevelled and cramped under the sloping roof, his glances at his watch, her ears constantly straining for any sounds from the rooms below. Both of them too tense for pleasure, but going through its rigours, him professionally, she dramatically.

Afterwards, when they had dressed again, they sat side by side on the bed like strangers in a doctor's waiting room, each thinking silently about how to end it, how to escape. She took his hand and held it on her lap, then began to speak.

'Your wife . . .'
'Catherine?'
'She sounded . . .'
'Yes?'
'She sounded . . .'
'Nice?'
'Yes. I . . .'
'I don't . . .'
'I can't . . .'
'I think that . . .'
'Me too.'

He sighed. She understood his sigh to mean that he didn't want to leave, and she sighed back at the thought that he might cancel his three o'clock lecture in order to stay. He had actually sighed because he was wondering how long he ought to stay to make it seem at least remotely respectable. He rested his eyes on the small wooden bookcase next to her bed. She had all the required texts as well as a rather unhealthy number of books by and about the American poet Sylvia Plath. This made him sigh again. She was trying very hard to imagine him back in his study, with the coffee cups on the window ledge and the view of the National Library and the letter trays overflowing with student essays, and she sighed again because now that she'd seen him in his underwear that seemed impossible.

He stood suddenly, ready to go, but somehow his watch had become entangled with her hair and she gave a yelp of pain as he unthinkingly yanked at it, ripping the hair from her head. They both looked aghast at the tangled clumps sprouting from the metal bracelet of his watch. He pulled at them, but they cut into his fingers and stretched and curled and slipped and clung until finally they snapped, leaving short tufts poking out here and there.

Tears had come to her eyes with the sudden pain. He looked at her and seeing this, with ill disguised irritation as much at himself, as with her, said 'I'm sorry,' then bluntly, 'Why don't you get that cut?'

That would have been the end of the story, except that some moments elusive as they may seem when lived, come back in other guises unbidden. Theirs was a photograph, unfortunately a very good photograph of a young girl on tip-toes, her long wet hair lifted wildly in the wind and a black coated man bent over her, his hands delicately cupping her upturned face as their lips met. Rain glistened on their faces and shone in silvery puddles on the paving stones at their feet, and behind them the sky was a black brooding mass of cloud.

It was a timeless image, a classic to be reproduced over and over, whose currency was love, truth and beauty. The people who bought the poster and the stationery range and the postcard assumed that it must have been posed, that it was really too perfect.

Magpie

Lucy's mother had often told her that while her sister Imogen was 'pretty', what Lucy had was 'personality'. Having 'personality' was tricky, thought Lucy—become too aware of it, and puff—it was gone, and you became awkwardly self-conscious and artificially exuberant. Lucy imagined it was something delicate, like a basket of eggs, which she had to constantly balance on her head. 'Pretty', on the other hand, was easy. As long as you had youth on your side, it was just there on the surface for everyone to see.

So Lucy grew up to envy and hate Imogen, and equally she learned to dislike her own image, to find nothing but faults and irregularities in the shape of her nose, the colour of her hair and eyes, the size of lips and chin and forehead.

'Oh, they're not at all alike are they?' distant aunts and neighbours would say, looking from one girl to the other, then letting their eyes linger admiringly on Imogen. As a child this had been the point when Lucy would do something funny; something to make them laugh. And they had laughed, but sometimes she resented their laughter, heard mockery in the musical sounds, the rise and fall of their voices. She'd grow suddenly solemn then, and wouldn't you know it? That would be funny too.

If Lucy found a fairy ring of toadstools she would wish that she was pretty. If she saw a shooting star she would wish that she had been an only child. If she saw one, two, three, four, five, six, seven, eight magpies she would wish that Imogen would disappear off the face of the earth.

When she was thirteen and Imogen was seventeen, the elder sister obeyed the call of her sibling's wishes, walked out one bright January morning and disappeared. Flew the nest.

And so tragedy descended on their home.

Their house, which was a replica of every other house in the street, with its bay windows and neat mock Tudor panelling in black and white, and its square topped hedges, its magnolia tree and snowdrops, traded its warm familiarity for one that was marked by a chill. Lucy felt it each time she unlatched the wooden gate and made her reluctant way up the path.

And just as tragedy had descended on this West London villa and its three occupants, so had love descended upon the head of their elder daughter, for Imogen was living in blissful and bohemian squalor just five miles away to the north east in Islington.

Imogen's leaving was as eloquent as a light being put out. But this would suggest that she, and she alone, had been capable of illuminating their lives. This was not the case, yet her absence was an obliterating cloud. Not knowing her fate was what eclipsed their lives and drove them to live in the gloaming.

Life goes on. As Lucy's father constantly says, 'Life must go on.' He always speaks as if Imogen were dead. He hints that she was too beautiful and good to live, calls her a borrowed angel. He's a true fatalist, a pessimist through and through. Lucy has never seen him weep. Not once. He expresses his emotions, when they erupt, in violence, but being a careful man, he releases these destructive energies by punching inanimate objects. Their once-immaculate house has a bruised and broken look about it. On the alcove wall, near the telephone, there's a fist-shaped dent. On the plastic panel near the side of the bath there's a large splintered crack where he kicked it bare-footed. The wardrobe in Imogen's room has a ragged hole where his hand went clean through.

There are old bloodstains near the scenes of these crimes. Lucy's father usually managed to do himself more damage than the object attacked. Part of the ritual was the blood letting, the silent frowning contemplation of the gashed knuckle; the rivulets of red tracing elegant patterns over his hand, down his arm.

Lucy's mother weeps. Mostly there is no noise. It is as

if the pain is trapped so deep inside her it cannot, must not escape. Her body shudders, the head nods strangely, tremulously, and her hands flutter as if batting away swarms of mite-sized demons.

Lucy's mother still goes about her daily schedule. She does the laundering, the vacuuming, the dusting, polishing and arranging of ornaments just as before, but she's become careless. She stumbles through the day blindly, leaving swathes of dust in geometric patterns where her zig-zagging stroke had missed. She knocks things over, and smashes her most precious china.

Flowers die in the vases and sit there week after week, the stems rotting and stinking in the stagnant water. The fruit bowls are full of shrunken, wrinkled apples, black bananas and mildewed oranges. The meals which the family sit down to eat every evening are always either burnt or half raw. The Hoover occasionally stands like a silent sentinel in the middle of the front room for days on end.

Lucy feels as if another of her childhood wishes has come true; she has become invisible. This, she feels, is her punishment.

She comes and goes; attends school, dreads Christmas and the long summer holidays. She buys clothes with money her father hands her from his wallet without even questioning her, without even looking in her eyes. She forges her parents' signatures on her unread report cards, begins to cook meals for herself; tins of soup or beans, or scrambled egg. She is careful to never laugh or show too much lightness of spirit. Hers is a half-life, a buried existence.

The years go by. Lucy becomes a woman, passes more 'O' levels than Imogen ever did. Grows up gracefully, matures without the acne that Imogen suffered, without the mood swings and the outbursts of tears and fury. Her face loses its roundness, stretches itself into an angular beauty.

She has become secretive and everyone around her

assumes this is shyness or studiousness, but really she is just waiting. Though for what, she cannot say.

Imogen, meanwhile, exists as though she were in a fairy tale; she is like an enchanted princess held by a bewildering spell. For Imogen, life is a beautiful dream.

Imogen sleeps on two mattresses, one on top of the other on the bare floor-boards in the attic room she shares with her boyfriend Tom. There is little else in the room, except for the old cast iron fireplace and the little window with the grey army blanket nailed up over it and the huge mirror which Tom found in a skip. Imogen gets her clothes from jumble sales. She dresses in crepe 1930's tea frocks and dyes her blonde hair raven black and has it cut in a bob because Tom says it makes her look like Louise Brooks.

For two years, Imogen has worked on a secondhand clothes stall at Portobello market. Tom usually stays at home reading American detective novels, because he says that they are the only really honest books he knows of and some day he's going to write one, and Imogen believes him, because she believes everything Tom tells her. Imogen reads them too, but half-heartedly as she feels she's missing something, as if her understanding weren't quite up to it.

Sometimes she starts to write a letter to her parents; 'Dear Mum and Dad and Lucy, Sorry it's taken so long to write, but . . .' and then she always gets stuck and doesn't know quite what to say. And besides, she is afraid that if they knew her whereabouts they would come steaming in and sweep her away. They'd carry her off and make her ordinary again, or make her 'as comfortably bourgeois as a force fed goose' as Tom puts it.

And, oh how terrible that would be! Tom would never love her then, not like he loves her now. And he does love her, because when she asked him he said, of course; he wouldn't be there otherwise. And his gruffness, she knows, is just his way.

One day (and wasn't this an event just waiting to

happen, even in a city as vast and populous as London), Lucy's best friend Vanessa sees Imogen at the market stall. She does not speak, just stares and stares at this ghost, this legend, this memory. This memory who is smiling so happily, and enjoying the golden autumn light on her skin, and taking money from a little green apron and counting out pound notes with such expertise.

Vanessa agonizes for almost a week with the knowledge of Imogen's existence, before deciding to act. She takes a reluctant Lucy to the market without explaining why. Lucy walks beside her, quiet and neat in her plaid skirt, her safe white blouse and sensible shoes.

Then Vanessa tugs her arm. 'Hang on,' she says, then 'Look.' They're behind a stall laden with old military paraphernalia; scarlet and khaki uniforms, World War 1 insignia and flags.

'What?' says Lucy.

'There, look,' Vanessa points, her arm and index finger an arrow that leads Lucy's eyes to something beyond the rifles and storm trooper helmets, to a young woman with shining black hair. Then as Lucy watches, the woman turns and Lucy sees, for the first time in four years, the face of her sister.

Lucy, ashen-cheeked, trailed by Vanessa, crosses the street. Imogen is smiling, laughing, talking animatedly. Lucy walks right up to her, stands facing her. Imogen gives Lucy the smile of a helpful shop assistant, and Lucy says aloud the word that she has silently lived with all these years.

'Why?' she says 'Why?'

Slowly recognition dawns on Imogen and she answers 'Lucy? Lucy? Oh, Lucy is it you?' But Lucy only repeats herself, 'Why?'

'Oh, Lucy,' says Imogen, and she reaches for Lucy as if to hug her.

'Why?' says Lucy, ducking away from the clutching arms.

And then Imogen, remembering at last that there was

once a life before this life, says 'I was in love. It was love. I was in love . . .' and she laughs nervously.

Imogen watched her sister walk away and wanted to run after her, but instead, she called 'I was in love, it was love.' But the word itself had somehow lost its meaning. It didn't matter how often she said it, or how much she wished for it, or how beautiful its sound, it was only in the end, the bitter-sweet warning song of a bird whose territory is threatened.

Running Away with the Hairdresser

The sun was shining that day, although there was also enough of a fresh breeze to send clouds skimming and chasing across the impossibly blue sky. At the top of Pen Bran we had watched the shadows of those clouds darken by turns the far hills and fields. Then, in those fleeting shadows, I detected nothing threatening; no hint of the trouble to come.

In the valley below us, running by the side of the river was the railway and, on the tracks, hurtling eastward towards England was a train. I watched it, I remember, full of longing. I wanted to escape even as I lay on the scrub grass of a Welsh mountainside with the girl I believed I loved in my arms.

The girl who, I thought, loved me. But instead of settling in the stillness of the moment, I was yearning for movement; for freedom, for the clouds' wild rampage away from the slumbering world.

She was married, and had a son. She'd brought him along that day. He was a pathetic scrap; six years old, lisping, stick-thin, freckled, and with hair so white, and eyes such a watery blue you'd have thought him an albino. He clung to her incessantly as if the wind might blow her away. And maybe he was right to detect the threat of some ancient and elemental force which plucked at her, and called her from their little home above the hairdressing shop, away from the town, the valley, and Wales, and into the dark underworld of England and beyond.

When she spoke to her son she called him, not by his name, but 'boy', as women in those parts often do. The boy was sulking and complaining of a headache, and whenever he said it, his eyes slid towards me accusingly, as though I were its chief cause.

'Come on, boy,' she said, sounding and looking more like a big sister than his mother, 'I'll race you to the top.'

But he grizzled all the more, like the bony bag of

misery he was. I didn't help matters much, I'll admit. I resented the sudden appearance of this mawkish creature, the restrictions he put on what we did during our brief time together. The watering down of our pleasures, the whispered words, the way she untangled my hand from hers whenever the kid was within a hundred yards.

We had precious little time together anyway, what with that hunkering, suspicious, ex-army husband of hers, and the hairdressing business with its rows of blue-rinsed old bags lined up beneath the dryers like overgrown turkeys under a grill; all gizzard-neck and gobble-gobble, and bulging, rolling eyes always on the look out for something to peck to death.

She was just twenty-two and only looked sixteen if she looked a day. I was thirty-eight, and a born liar. I told her I was twenty-nine, thus placing myself in the same decade as her. She never guessed the truth.

I had never married, and secretly, I had decided that I was never going to get tied down like that. If she assumed otherwise, well then, that was her problem.

I still smoked back then, which is yet another clue to my state of mind—even at almost forty I thought that I was going to live forever.

All of her energy was going into entertaining the boy. They were careening over the hill, plucking daisies and making long chains and winding themselves up in them. I lay back on my elbows, with ankles crossed and a Player's Number 6 stuck in the corner of my mouth, squinting at the sun and letting the frown stay creased between my brows even when the sun went in.

'You're sulking, aren't you?'

She was standing over me, I remember, and the sun gaped blindingly over her left shoulder. The boy had wandered off in search of bigger daisies. She kicked at the sole of my shoe, 'You're bloody jealous of 'im aren't you?'

'Grow up!' I snarled, 'Get a grip, for Christsake.'

She pulled a face, then turned to check on the kid's

whereabouts. I took my chance and launched myself at her ankles, and grappled her down. We'd messed around like this before, giggling and tickling one another and play-wrestling, and I was laughing, except that I could detect a hollow edge to the sound. And she wasn't laughing at all.

It was in those seconds that all our dreams began to crack and distort at the edges like a snapshot left to bake for a whole summer on a window ledge. I was still laughing my hollow laugh, still caught in the pretext of affectionate play, when her elbow smashed into my nose; hard enough to stun me and hard enough to produce a few droplets of thin snotty blood.

'Bitch!' I said, and a few other things besides. I rolled away from her, and blinked and snorted like a scolded dog who's been whacked on the snout with a newspaper.

She was up and running, and for once, calling the boy's name. 'Hugh!' she yelled. 'Hugh!' over and over, until it no longer sounded like a name or a word you would recognize, but some she-animal's mating call.

We both heard the splash. It was sudden and it was out of place; there was no water nearby that we could see, and for all those reasons and more it was frightening.

Her cries now took on an even more breathless and distorted quality as she raced toward the sound with me at her heels. We got there while ripples of black water were still making hypnotic circles around the space where the boy had fallen in. You could see how the land had collapsed in on itself, how years of earth and grass had knotted themselves together into a conspiracy that hid the empty air of an old mine shaft and the underground pool it led to. I stood there marvelling at it, noting the fringed grass at its edges and the lace-like display of roots that were so diagrammatically exposed, and feeling the chill of the cold air that rose up from the water.

Then, rousing me at last from my reverie, I saw from the corner of my eye that she was taking off her shoes and socks, shaking off her jacket.

'You can't swim,' I said, kicking off my shoes, and for

a second we were both tearing at our clothes like hungry lovers in some passionate race against time. I won the race, and bare feet first, I was swallowed by, first the air, and then the water. I went down fast, blind and shocked into the engulfing cold, then came up for air, and then went under again with eyes open at the stinging dark, and precious little time in my lying poisoned lungs.

I couldn't find him. I came up again, gasping and treading water and not even daring to look up to where she stood. The third time I went under seemed the longest. I went down as far as I dared, but found nothing solid there, no silty bed or rocks or debris and no half-drowned boy either.

My mind, however, was playing tricks with me. Perhaps it was the shock or the fear or the cold that caused it. Whatever it was doesn't matter actually, all I know is that while I swam around down there, I suddenly felt very calm. Happy, almost. And I thought about three things. The first was a song, which I suppose, I seemed to hear rather than actually think about in any concrete way. It was playing in my head like a film soundtrack. It was The Spencer Davies Group's 'Keep on Running' and the words seemed to me like directions for that very instance in my life, 'Keep on running,' they said 'keep on hiding'.

At the same time I had a sort of vision of myself running down the High Street in the sunshine, and she was running with me; she was by my side holding my hand and we didn't care who saw us, or who knew about us, or anyone or anything, because we were gone, and out of there and never coming back. But as I swam and ran, and as my lungs grew tighter and more desperate for air, I lost my grip on her hand. Growing weak, my hand was spasmodically pumping the watery nothingness in search of her lost dream hand when it finally found the thin half-dead reality of his.

It should have been a moment of triumph; of relief, of heroism, of everything that is good and sweet and noble, but instead of that, one evil and corrupting idea leapt on me like a water serpent in the deep. The idea was that I should leave him there, that he was dead already and I needed to save myself. It was a tragic accident and I had done all I could, and I could not be blamed, and she would be free, we would be free. And I saw the boy's life stretching into the future and deemed it a sickly sad future, not worth living.

It is not a memory I am proud of. I could blame all kinds of temporary madness brought on by the lack of oxygen. I might even conjure up some evil supernatural force infecting my mind, a jealous ghost, a spiteful water baby, alien forces of destruction, but these would only be vague excuses, a thin veneer of lies which could do nothing to save me, or salve the wounds of terrible self knowledge. And the truth was I wanted him dead. Not just because I felt that his death would free us, but also because, like some ancient jealous God I wanted to destroy him and thus weaken her.

Then I felt a movement from the boy and without thought, I found myself swimming, swimming upwards, with him hooked under one arm and the daylight like the phosphorescence from an angel's wing calling us home, and back to the world.

I have told no-one of this. Instead I have spent the best part of sixteen years running. But in the end, I ran away alone. The vision which I had of the two of us was only that; a vision as illusory as a dream.

The running away does not make me free however much it gives that impression. The running away is my curse, my punishment for darker sins, even if those sins were never quite acted on. They may have been left there in Wales, in a dark gash on the hill's surface, in the ripples of a secret pool, but part of me remains tangled among them; the soul's foot caught forever in weeds.

MIKE JENKINS

Some Kind o' Beginning

The sound o' voices rises from-a street. More banterin 'an arguin, but it still brings back tha night. There's too many thin's remind me. Ev'ry time I see Dave on telly playin fer-a Jacks. Ev'ry time I go out to a Club (though tha int often nowadays) an there's a barney.

Puttin on my face, layer 'pon layer, I carn elp thinkin ow she must afta dollop it on t' cover over wha I done. An there by my mirror is-a cuttin. People might think I'm sick or summin, but I jus don' wanna forget. It's a warnin: NEVER AGEN!

Wish I wuz goin out with them girls. Theyr jokin pierces-a glass an ruffles-a curtains. A whool gang of em, I bet, like we woz in Merthyr, me, Nadine, Andrea an Jayne (with a "y" don' forget, she'd say). I long fer theyr voices now, goin up an down like-a mountains an valleys. Funny tha', it's flatter down yer an-a way 'ey talk ave not got the same music to it some'ow.

Mascara, face cream . . . owever much I put on, I could never be like er. My teeth stick out in funny ways an I got ooded eye-lids like my dad wuz an owl or summin. I light up a fag an burn an ole jest above er ead. I 'member wha ee once said, 'Martine, I'm sorry t' tell yew, but yewr breath's mingin . . . Yew should try an give up.' But all em months in the Centre I needed em so much. I'll never stop now, not even if I seen im agen.

The thin's the papers said, an mostly true I know. But oo cun understand all 'at goadin? All 'at gangin up an pickin on me er friends done? It wuz like Cardiff 'gainst-a Jacks, we all knew it wuz gunna go off sometime, but no-one spected I would make it appen.

I blow smoke at er picture. The eadlines blur. I yer my flat-mate Chrissie come in from work: tidy job in-a Travel Agents, all dolled up. She's like me, tryin t' make a new life. She've ad 'n ard time, brought up in-a Omes. Carn understand ow she's so straight-lined though. TV on, cuppa tea next . . .

'Hey, Martine! D'you want a cuppa?'

'No ta, Chrissie! I'm off soon!'

She knows all 'bout me, but it don't bother er. She reckons er dad done worse thin's than tha to er an er mam.

Tha bloody burn above er air looks like a friggin alo! I feel like ashin tha photo once an fer all, but instead I stub-a fag out on-a mirror, right where my teeth jut out comical.

Chrissie looks so relaxed in-a sittin room when I enter, feet up an sippin away. As she turns er head fer a moment she reminds me of er, tha beaky nose an pointy chin, but . . .

'Martine, you look great!' she says, an I do feel ready t' face the world, even though I wan' more.

'Aye, but oo cares in tha poncy otel?'

'Well, maybe you'll meet someone tonight. Some millionaire soccer star'll be passing through and propose to you over his lasagne!'

'Soccer star?'

'Oh . . . sorry Martine!'

I larf an she wriggles in er chair an echoes me. Soon it's 'S'long!' and 'Bye'. Me wonderin ow she cun talk so posh with er background an ave survived.

The streets o' Abernedd turnin inta Merthyr by the second. Cack-jumpin an spottin where yesterday's shops ewsed t' be. See-through windows replaced by-a environmentally-friendly sort, perfect fer graffiti an posterin. Local bands like Panic Stations an The Pocket Billiards advertisin gigs. I woz inta football when my friends listened t' the Merthyr equivalents o' them. I woz turned on when Merthyr played the Jacks (Dave wern with em 'en) an stood with Dazzy an the boys chantin an loathin to a pitch where I lost myself.

Wassa time? Shit! Four minutes late an moany ol cow Thorpe'll be bound t' dock me.

Car beeps me. Two boys in overalls, all over painty. Give em a V and see em mouthin off at me.

There it is at bloody last, The Dog and Duck, Abernedd's finest, 3 star, AA. Looks real tidy from-a front an all, but I could blow it open, wha with ol Thorpey an is stingy ways . . . scrapin-a mould off of fruit an tha ol can-opener sheddin rust!

'Yer! Wha's this in my peas, waitress?'

'Oh, I believe it's some sort o' garnish, sir.'

When in doubt, call it garnish, tha's wha ee tol us t' say.

Just as I'm gaspin fer a fag an fumblin in my pockets, Thorpey ops through-a door t' greet me.

'Martine, you're five minutes late again. It'll have to stop, Marteen!'

Sayin my name like I woz 'n alien. Feel sorry fer is missis, I do. Imagine im on top on the job . . . 'You've had your ten seconds heavy-petting, dear. Now we'd better hurry up and start breathing faster!'

'Marteen! Stop grinning and get ready, will you!'

Soon I'm all frilled up an layin-a tables, all-a time chattin t' Michelle oo on'y jes started las week an oo keeps cockin ev'rythin up. She's so nervous an tryin t' please, but Thorpey give er so much jip when she wrote-a orders down wrong, she nearly give up on er first day. An the bloke what ad steak 'n' kidney pie 'stead o' steak! I thought ee wuz gonna crack er one on-a spot!

Lee, the main chef, ee takes-a piss outa Mich no end. Ee tried it with me when I begun, so I tol Mich t' take no notice. But she don' know when ee's bullin or not. Ee tol er the correct way t' serve chips wuz with a fork an she believed im. By-a time she'd got em on-a plate, they'd frozen agen!

Friday evenin, but it's real quiet. I serve a family with a stroppy veggie wife an two kids insistin on avin adult portions.

'What's this Vegetable Steak Casserole?' she asks.

'Oh no,' I says, 'tha's vegetable casserole with steak in it.'

'But it does say Vegetable Steak, doesn't it?'

This coulda gone on forever, on'y er ol man tells er t' ave-a veggie lasagne.

Lee's outa is ead as per usual. I reckon ee's on summin, I do.

'One veggie lasagne, but I reckon there's some rat in it somewhere, Martine . . . Look! There's its brother!' ee yells, pointin is spatula at-a corner of-a kitchen. I twirl round like a ballerina, then give im a shove in is bulbous beer-gut an ee makes out t' swat me like a fly. Mich comes in lookin all excited like she seen some lush popstar. She catches old o' my arm, while I'm on-a look-out fer ol Thorpey, oo always seems t' rush in when we int workin tidy.

'Martine! There's these really ace boys! . . . Yew gotta come an give me an and! I'm on pins!'

'Aye, I will, arfta I done this one table. Okay?'

So I takes in the veggie lasagne an the usband's omemade pie (what comes straight from-a freezer) an ave a gawk. There's a loada tables put together an, jest as Mich said, a pile o' stonkin men and boys in posh suits an flash ties. Then I see Thorpey chattin to an older man oo wuz with em an ee glares over at me, so I make out I'm busy servin the famlee.

As I'm dishin out-a veg, I yer a Merthyr voice an 'n unmistakable one at tha. I practically fling-a veg onto the bloke's lap an spatter im with gravy. The back end o' Dave's ead, I'm shewer.

'Excuse me!' says the bloke.

'Oh, I'm sorry!' I grovel, in case ee should call Thorpey. I do a rapid runner back to-a kitchen an grab old o' Mich, oo's gotta andfull o' prawn cocktails.

'Well, Martine, what d'yew think, eh?'

'Mich! Lissen! There's this boy I ewsed t' know there . . . I think theyr Swonzee football team . . . I gotta do the next servin, right?'

Coz I'm so igh-pitched an wound up, Lee yers me over is sizzlin chip-oil an steak-bashin. Is face is a pumpkin grin.

'Ne' mind the rat, where's the fuckin poison? I could never stick the Jacks!'

'Don' be darft, Lee. Ee's from Merthyr.'

'Ey, Mart, I thought yew were a true Bluebird.'

'Tha's all in-a past . . . Right, Mich, give us them prawn cocks!'

Michelle's nearly creamin er knicks on-a spot, she's so worked up.

'Ey, we could be on yer . . . I fancy the big black one, I do!'

'I gotta black puddin in the fridge, if yew don't get off with im,' shouts Lee.

'Shurrup Lee, y' racist dick!' I yell as Mr Thorpe comes bustin through-a door. Ee's tampin an is ard white face its me like a breeze-block.

'Martine,' ee whispers snakey, 'just get on with the job or you're out! Right?'

I feel like tellin im t' stuff it, but I iss back 'Yes Mr Thorpe!' I go calm but quick inta the dinin area an make a point o' servin Dave first. I glance over t' see Mich urryin towards the big black fella, oo looks real chuffed. Dave's busy talkin, so I lean right over im, cranin t' face im like I wuz goin t' give im a peck.

'Yewr prawn cocktail sir!' I says, so deliberate an sarky ee turns straight away, lookin curious till ee recognises me. Is eyes 'n mouth narrow t' three blades. Then ee turns away with a flick o' is ead like ee wuz eadin-a ball or summin.

As I return to-a kitchens I yer im callin me back. I don' wanna respond, but thinkin o' Thorpey's warnin, I decide to.

'Uh . . . scuse me, waitress, but can I ave my steak well done, please? I carn stand the sight o' blood!'

An all-a players larf, like it woz some private joke.

'Yes, of course sir!' I feel like spittin out-a words, but I control myself, savin it up. Inside, I'm so angry coz ee treated me like I woz nobody. All is indifference brings it back: ow ee ewsed me against er, er against me. I seen ow ee wanted us t' be total enemies. An I played is game orright . . . a Stanley knife I on'y brung fer protection . . . she wuz avin a go at me all-a time . . . 'Martine, yew've lost im, yew bitch! Le's face it, yewr a loser!' . . . Blood everywhere. Now I gotta remember. Er blood on my clothes an ands: I knew I'd never wash off them stains. An when Dave says bout is steak jes then it seemed aimed, like is sharp eyes shinin.

I decide t' take in these special steak knives we aven ewsed frages an Lee thinks I'm darft.

'Wha yew wanna bother with em for? I need em f' choppin up the rats anyway.'

'Lee do me favour an chop yewrself up, they'll be one less rat then.'

I rub my and cross-a blade o' one. I feel scared an thrilled at-a same time. Mich comes in grinnin all over er body, as if she've orready got tha fella. I old up-a knife towards er.

'Ey, Martine! Go easy! I never spoke to yewrs. Onest!'

'It's okay, Mich. This one's fer im!' I clatter-a knives onto a tray, leavin Michelle stunned.

This time I take it real slow, as if I woz strokin. I know wha I'm doin, so's I ask oo's avin steak an watch is face as I carefully place each knife. I old each one a while before puttin it down an I cun see is panic risin. Ee cun see I'm leavin im till last an ow much I'm relishin it all. Looks as if ee's shittin is load when I finally come t' im.

'Yew avin steak, sir . . . Well done, wern it?'

'Er . . . aye . . . ta,' ee tries t' act so cool, but is ands 're fiddlin with is other cutlery, as if ee's searchin f' weapons!'

I take old o' the las steak-knife an prepare t' show im. Now ee'll get the message. I cun take down tha cuttin. I cun wash off tha red. I sweep the knife up to is face an ee jerks back in is chair, nearly fallin. At-a same time, Michelle comes in screamin, 'Don' do it, Martine! Don' do it agen!'

An I says t' Dave, real calm . . . 'Is this done enough fer yew sir?'

Ever'thin appens so quick, I think I've sliced im

without knowin. Is team-mates 're laughin, Michelle grabs my arm an Thorpey's fussin an pullin me back t' the kitchen. Ee drags me outa the door inta the yard. I still gotta knife, but there's no blood anywhere t' be seen.

'This is no joke, Martine! How dare you treat our customers like this? Who do you think you are? You can't . . .'

I fling the knife to the ground an-a sound severs is words, leaves em angin.

'Yew cun stick yewr bloody job, Mr Thorpe! I wozn messin, fer yewr information, it wuz fer real. I owed tha boy one!'

'I should never have taken you on . . . I knew about your record, you know . . . They told me you'd changed . . . Now, get out of my hotel!'

I undo-a apron an scrumple it up as ee shoves past me. I fling it in-a bin an feel a real buzz, though ee never seen me.

As I stride away down-a street, a coach passes an faces stare at me with a 'Wow' on theyr lips. All of em 'cept one, that is. I lost so much to im: my body, my freedom an now my job. I'll go ome an take-a scissors to er photo. Cut it up inta tiny pieces knowin tha won' be the end, but tha problee, this is some kind o' beginnin.

Wanting to Belong

Hiya! I'm Gary Crissle and this is my story, well some of it. I know my name sounds like rissole and rhymes with gristle, but if you're smirking you wouldn't if you saw me, cos I'm pretty solid, as they say round Cwmtaff. I've got boxer's muscles and I'm tall as a basketball star.

Gary is short for Gareth. I like Gary because it's more cool. Gareth sounds a bit naff, though it makes me more Welsh. It wasn't like a passport when I first came to Cwmtaff though. It didn't matter to them.

I got Gareth from my mam, who comes from here originally. She's small and blonde and nothing like you'd picture a typical Welsh woman to be. She met my dad at a disco in Cambridge. It must've been dark cos he isn't exactly John Travolta. More like John Revolter, I'd say!

The Crissle comes from my dad of course, and isn't the only thing he's lumbered me with. There's my teeth, which stick out like a cartoon rabbit, though my brace has trained them down recently. The first month at Pencwm Comp, I had it on. Imagine being from England and having an iron mouth as well. The stick I got was beyond. I never told anybody the name of the village I'm from, as it would give them more ammunition. It's called Horseheath. They'd have me born in a cowpat! So Cambridge was enough for me. When people talk about racism, I know it isn't all black and white.

(*I'm writing now when I can. There's a terrible routine to my life, but it helps to get things down.*)

It seems that Mark Rees was behind most of it. Sparky they called him. He was a small, scrawny boy into everything he shouldn't have been. Most kids in my class worshiped him, while most teachers couldn't stand him.

Sparky loathed me from the start. He was always nicking my bag and hiding it, so in the end I stopped bringing one to school. He got the others to go 'Oo arr!

Oo arr!' whenever I read in class and even called me 'A posh twat' which is a joke cos my accent is real country, though I've picked up some Cwmtaff recently.

The crunch came when Sparky and his gang decided to jump me on my way home. He didn't like the way I was friendly with the teachers. He thought I was a crawler, a grass, but I never meant anything. I just wanted to belong.

Well, my mam was working all hours and my dad's job at Hoover's was on the line. Things were very strained in my house and I snapped at school that day. Although I'm strapping I'm not a troublemaker, but Mark Rees pushed me too far.

We had this supply teacher with a fancy voice, who was also from England. I felt sorry for him but couldn't sit there like a stuffed parrot while our set played up. He tried to make contact when he heard me, and I replied to be polite.

'Who do you support?'

'Cambridge United. They're great!'

'Oo 're they? Oo 're they? Oo 're they?' Sparky started up a chant that all his mates copied and the poor wimpy supply screamed 'SHUT UP!' as sweat leapt from his face.

I lost my head. I clutched the paper in front of Sparky (with only the drawing of a magpie on it), crumpled it up and rammed it into his gob.

'Out!' yelled the supply, 'both of you. Out!'

I suppose he thought he was being fair, but what happened after was that a Deputy, Mr Lloyd, found us in the corridor mouthing and shoving each other, and he blamed Mark Rees cos he'd got a reputation worse than Ian Wright.

I didn't expect him to get revenge so soon. Him and his mates ambushed me in one of the alleys in Penôl estate, where we both lived. I didn't stand a chance against six of them, though I tried my best.

'Bog off back to bleedin England!' Rees swore as he kicked me to the ground.

I made out I was hurt more than I was by yelling hell and this woman stuck her head over her fence to give off to Sparky's mob. They gobbed at her and left me blacker than a copper's uniform and bleeding like a beaten boxer. The woman was nice and offered me a cuppa. I told her no and stumbled home.

There were plenty in school who didn't go along with Sparky, who knew he'd end up going down or killing himself in some stolen car. But in my form he ruled like one of the Mafia. His word was law.

I began to really resent my mother for being Welsh and for dragging us back here. My younger brother in Year 7 seemed to be having it easy though, cos he was sickeningly good at everything. He was called Ryan and was a left-winger and they nicknamed him 'Giggsy'.

I wanted to impress upon Sparky and the boys that I wasn't a swot. As my schoolwork went downhill faster than a freewheeling pushbike, my mam got a warning letter home. She threatened to ground me for at least a month that evening.

'I ain't staying in!'

'Go to yewer room, Gary!'

'I ate this crappy town and I wanna get back so I can see United every ome game. It's your fault!'

'Yewr dad'll ammer yew when ee gets ome. Now do as yew're tol!'

'Naff off woman!'

I slammed out and ran for my freedom. I ran towards town through streets which were carbon-copies. I ran past the bus-shelter where Siân Jones and her friends stood smoking. I liked Siân, but the girls she bothered with bugged me no end.

'Ey Gary, wha's up? Runnin from Sparky agen?' They cackled like demented chickens. Siân looked on, sad.

I didn't have a clue where I was going. All I ever did in the evening was have a kick around with Ryan and his friends. I thought of getting on a bus or train, but I was skint.

(*Listen, I've got to go now and leave this for a while. Unfortunately, there are things to be done. Lights to be put out. Promise I'll be back.*)

Anyway, what did I do? I carried on striding down High Street, till I heard this familiar voice calling out—'Gary! Gazza!'

Gazza? Was it really referring to me?

And there, sitting on a bench was Sparky, ready for the taking if I'd been in the mood. He was a tiny ant without his gang: could easily be stamped on. I crossed over to him, more out of curiosity than anything. His eyes were glassy and he giggled for no reason. I could see how other kids were attracted to his cheeky eyes.

'Alright? Where's the rest then?'

'Revisin f' the exams, o' course.' I could see he was talking bull cos of his grin. 'Ow come yew're down yer. Not yewer scene.'

'I've ad enough. I'm runnin away!' Strangely, I found myself speaking like him.

'This is-a cheapest way t' excape, Gary.'

He took out a carrier-bag from under the bench and offered it. It contained a flagon. Sparky was a real alkie.

'What is it, meths?'

'Scrumpy Jack. On'y the ard suff. Knock it back!'

He was standing now and practically pouring it down my throat. Before I knew it we were exchanging swigs and strutting through town. 'Lookin f' action,' Sparky said, though it was deserted as a wet winter Sunday.

'Don' worry Gaz, there's always one fuckin plank-ead!'

I didn't know what he was on about, but the Scrumpy was doing its business and I was travelling far enough without spending a thing. I liked the way Sparky had changed towards me, though I couldn't fathom why. Maybe it was the booze. If so, I didn't want to be around when he got a hangover.

As we passed the taxi-rank and the station, he was babbling away like he did in lessons.

'Gary, yew carn elp bein English. Listen. I really liked

the way yew stuffed tha paper down my gob. Yew got style. We could be a team.'

He began to sound like some gangster film. Nothing seemed real till we reached the rough and ready car-park near the railway line. Then he spotted something and flung the bag into a tangle of weeds.

'Looks as if someone's missed theyr train from Cardiff.'

His baseball cap was a buzzard's beak, as he clawed in his jeans pocket. What he'd noticed in the distance was one particular car, not a new job, but an Escort GT all the same. I could make that out and I was no expert.

When he took out a screwdriver I was dead scared. In fact, I was nearly pooping my boxers! The cider hadn't made me bold enough, but I couldn't let on or Sparky would spread it round school faster than teletext. Instead, I made out I was a professional.

'Ow about goin fer a better one?' I suggested, hoping he'd be diverted.

'No way, Gazza. This one's got no bells. Yew int scared, 're yew?' He stared, grin gone, eyes full of purpose.

'No way! Let's go for it then!'

'Yew wan-oo?' He held out the screwdriver.

'No thanks. You're the best, Sparky. Everybody says.'

I thought of legging it rapidly, but before I could say 'Yer come the cops!' he was into the Escort and he even had a key.

'C'mon, Oo Ar ol son. Le's mule!'

He called me Oo Ar pleasantly now. I felt accepted. As soon as I sat in the passenger seat his put his foot down and screamed away like the cops were chasing us already. I belted up, but didn't feel exactly safe. Joy-riding's definitely not the word for it. I'd call it 'mental muling', except I'm not sure what that means.

He drove like a boy possessed, taking the roundabouts by the Labour Club almost on two wheels. We flew under the railway bridge and out of town. The cider wore off in seconds. I knew he was more than half gone and though he handled the car like a bucking bronco, I could still see us getting thrown.

'Jus drop me off at ome fer a change of pants!' I gasped.

Luckily, the road was deserted as town had been. Everything was fast forward and my hands fumbled the dashboard for a hold button.

'Where we goin, Sparky?' I asked, trying to sound super-cool.

'Oo knows? An oo fuckin cares!'

Then he lifted both hands and I closed my eyes and—

(*Interruptions! There are always people poking their noses in here. I'll start my story again when I can. But with all the commotion going on I don't know when.*)

I opened them and we were on the slip-road overtaking a lorry. Sparky was yelping and laughing his head off at me.

'I cun smell summin, Gaz, an it int the engine burnin!'

'Now what? The cops are bound to find out an I'll be for it. My dad'll murder me!'

'Right! Jes round Asda's roundabout, through Macdonald's fer a burger an 'en ram-raid a gypo camp.'

'No way, Sparky, there'll be a huge great security barrier.'

'I ate em!'

'What? Security barriers?'

'Na, gypos! Worse 'an the English. No offence like.'

He sped round Blaenmorlais top and back downhill again. I saw a white car along the Heads of the Valleys which could've been the police.

'Spark! Look! I'm sure I seen the cops!'

'I'll go up Bogey Road. We'll lose em tha way.'

He took a sharp left and I had to admire his skill. It was a Grand Prix to him.

'Better 'an shaggin, eh? Even with Siân!'

Suddenly, it was all ugly. I noticed the glint in his eyes when he mentioned her. I wondered what the hell I was doing in a stolen car with a boy whose gang had only recently jumped me. I didn't belong here either. He drove frantically towards the unofficial gypsy camp with its wooden fence. My dad had driven past once and my mam told me about it.

He swerved into the entrance and I instantly made a grab for the wheel. He jammed on the brakes, skidded and we hit the fence and a man standing just behind it. He fell with the impact as the car stopped.

Sparky reversed and accelerated up the hill, yelling a series of curses at me. Now he was truly mad and veered off the road onto the moors, our headlights picking out fleeing sheep and small ponies trying to gallop away.

'Orsemeat f' supper, Gary? Yew aven ad Siân 'en, I take it? Yew mus be the on'y one!'

The Escort rose, then dipped wildly into a pit. My body jerked like a fit. I couldn't see! Sparky shouted so loudly and painfully it razored my nerves. The car was motionless. I could feel damp spreading. I daren't open my eyes this time. I wanted to wake up somewhere else: at home, in comfort, by the telly. I wanted to rewind the tape and delete what had happened since I met Sparky.

Everything was frighteningly quiet. I kept on seeing that man we'd knocked over like a wooden pole, maybe lying dead.

If only I hadn't touched the wheel. Then I imagined Sparky and Siân Jones at it in the back of a car like this, and dared open my eyes again.

My jeans were blood-soaked. It was on my hands. I wasn't cut. Where was the blood . . ? Sparky embraced the steering-wheel. His head was deeply cut. I whispered 'Sparky' and shook him. No reply. His face was deathly white. I panicked. Releasing the belt, I staggered out. I stumbled back along the direction I thought we'd come, tripping over clumps of reed. Surely the road wasn't far? Luckily, it was a clear night. I swore and swore at Mark Rees, for every step a different word. I nearly crossed the road without realising it. A pile of tipped rubbish told me it was there. I followed it downwards and heard ahead another voice of panic, echoing mine.

I'd have to pass that camp and they could kill me, but

it was my only chance of getting help. Maybe Sparky could be saved. I didn't know if I wanted him to be, but I'd have to try.

What could I tell them? What convincing story? I groped in the dark for one.

In the end, I didn't have a chance to explain. As I trudged towards the ramshackle camp among what looked like waste-heaps, all I could hear was—'Look yer's one! Quick, grab im!'

Before I knew it a horde of youths and children were coming for me. I went on, shouting 'Elp, elp! I need an ambulance, quick!'

There must've been blood on my face as well, cos they held back from attacking me. The young men grabbed my arms, the children my jeans, as if making a citizen's arrest and marched me towards a battered old van, parked over our skid-marks. Among cries for revenge like 'Give im a boot in the goolies!' I noticed how one man, who was holding open the back doors of the van, managed to pacify them.

'Sure he's hurt. Leave him be!'

His voice was authority. I was chucked like a sack of coal into the back alongside the old man we'd knocked over, who lay groaning between two rolls of carpet. My head hit a sharp jutting edge of metal and began to bleed. I welcomed the pain. I deserved it. Absurdly, I began to wish I'd been injured more seriously.

'It wasn't me! I wasn't drivin!' I explained pathetically to the man who drove the van, who'd saved me from the mob.

(*I can hear someone coming. I'm going to tell those kids to 'Bog off or I'll kick your eads in!'*)

It's later now and I'll tell you what happened. Bri, my Care Assistant came in. He saw me writing.

'Good news, Gar . . . Oh, sorry! Wha's this then? Yew doin omework? I don' believe it!'

I rolled up this paper hurriedly, holding it tight, in case

he decided to investigate. I've got a lot of time for him, but he does want to know everything.

'It's nothin, Bri. Jus letters, tha's all.'

'Okay! Anyway,' he says, eying me suspiciously, 'yewr parents want yew back an I think there's a really good chance of it appenin . . . everyone knows yew've done yewr time in yer. T' be onest, it woz an ard deal in the first place.'

Brian put his hand on my shoulder and I had to swallow hard to keep down the tears. I squinted into the mirror and observed myself, thin and puny, for the first time genuine. Perhaps I should change my story? I wanted to hug him and tell him I'd never do anything like it again, but I couldn't be so soft even in my room with no-one watching.

'Thanks, Bri,' I said, thinking of Sparky half-dead in hospital and with a chair-bound future ahead of him, and of others like him who'd go from probation, to fines, to prison. I thought of that old gypsy in his grimey, cast-off suit rattling agony in the van, each moan my guilt. I thought of his family who forgave me while I sat with them all night, willing the monitor to keep on bleeping his life.

I'll end it now, though I'm sure there are bits I've left out. Do I belong in Cwmtaff? Well, I know where I don't belong that's for sure.

Allotment for Memories

You wouldn't think these lumps on the earth I'm standing on concealed so much, would you? I mean, they're smooth and firm as a greyhound's back and seem part of the landscape, but really all they are is overgrown slag-heaps.

About a week ago I came here. Sometimes I come to escape, at others just to gaze down on the town and think. The office where I work shrinks to Lego and I wish it could be dismantled as easily. My missis prefers the forestry path. At least it's going somewhere, she'd say. Here, I'm standing still on history, on tons of coal owned by Celtic Power, or whatever they call the company now. That's typical, she would say. But she doesn't know because, the thing is, this is my private place, an allotment for memories. I nurture them carefully. From out of the black-patched moors comes my father, a stern yet guiding presence. His strong sense of the power of history handed down, especially those tales of local heroes defying their Masters, risking all for vital ideals and pennies. If this land were dug up for an opencast mine I'd have to move away.

Yes, last week was definitely escape. We were on the verge of real conflict, where vases would fly and we'd say things we'd later regret, but never admit to being sorry. As always, the week's chores built up, so the house resembled a laundry, dust accumulated so even the spiders moved out in disgust and our carpets had more crumbs than the bird-table.

'Malcolm!' The full name treatment meant TROUBLE. 'Yew don' even notice, d' yew? Yew'd live in a skip if it ad a telly.'

'An 'n aerial . . .'

'Tha's it! Joke! Yewr answer t' ev'rythin! I give up!'

So I ran out here in desperation, stumbling over the tussocky surface, coat half on and shoe-laces undone.

Here, where I couldn't be seen from our back window. My own middle-aged den.

But as I approached these twmps I could hear giggling, sighing and animated chatter. From the top of this tip I peered down to see—in brazen daylight—a young couple canoodling. Well, they were more than canoodling, I'd say, because he was on top of her and both were shedding clothes faster than skinny-dippers. I glimpsed his hand scurrying like a small animal finding a warm resting place.

I breathed heavily from the exertion and both of them stopped their antics to stare in my direction. A bird rose from behind me—a meadow pipit, I believe—and they seemed to ignore me, following its flight and song a moment before resuming.

I rushed away downhill, alongside the course of one of the many streams. I headed for what is known locally as 'The Chartist's Stone', though my father believed it had nothing to do with them. It's a large, incongruous boulder, like something deposited by the Ice Age. You could certainly imagine those Chartists orating from its natural platform, but to me it was a point of contact with my son. (He was away at uni. and too busy making enough money to survive during holidays, so we didn't see him often). When he was a toddler we'd go there to play 'King of the Castle'. I remember once tumbling downslope so authentically he chased after me, concerned and calling 'Dad, dad! Yew okay? I didn' urt yew, did I?' After I got up, laughing, he decided to try the same ploy. However, he failed to stop himself rolling and I chased after him, only just catching hold before he fell into a brook.

On my way back, I approached these tips warily, drawn to the possibility of that couple, yet not wanting them to discover me spying and think me some 'dirty old man'. That vision disturbed me, as if I'd seen it on some film or in a dream.

As I reached the slight ridge I was both relieved and disappointed to find they'd gone. I decided to investigate their cwtch in the hillside, after all it was like they'd invaded my territory. Their clothes were probably smeared by tell-tale coal, which cropped up between the heather and grass and they might arouse suspicions when they got home.

I noticed something lying in the long reeds near where they'd been. Probably a used condom, or some other item of lust. They treated it all like a game, these young people: no notion of the consequences.

Getting closer I made out a fine, old-fashioned head-scarf. Were they back in? I certainly hadn't noticed and, having no daughter, was out of touch. Picking it up, I saw it was creamy, delicately-patterned and had a hint of perfume. I smoothed it and whispered 'I wish . . .' as though I could release some genie. I have to admit it, it stirred something in me, its silkiness like a piece of lingerie.

I hid it in my inside coat-pocket. It seemed strangely familiar. Had Shirley Maclaine (my all-time favourite actress) discarded it in the street in 'Days of Wine and Roses', to be ravished by the wind?

When I returned, Rachel had calmed down and now a glowering silence replaced her previous malice. I'd done nothing wrong, but knew I was to blame. I'd been a huge disappointment to her. She'd always desired to get away from this valley, to see other worlds. Now she sat dug-deep in a novel, as I ghosted past without a greeting, knowing talk was pointless.

Upstairs, I took out the head-scarf and held it next to my face, inhaling a feeling of being young, full of vibrancy. I couldn't recall ever having been so adventurous with Rachel. Continents away in thought, Rachel gave me a shock by bursting in and dumping my shirts on our bed.

'Wha? Wherever did you find tha, Malcolm? It carn be! Tha's incredible!'

'Ow? Ow d'yew mean?'

She lifted it and shook it out, reviving it from a deep sleep.

'This Malcolm . . . don' yew remember? Yew bought it

f' me in Morgan's, when we woz courtin. I ewsed t' wear it all-a time. Always thought I'd lost it outa back there . . . it's amazin!'

'No . . . it woz in a box at the top of the cupboard. I woz lookin f' photos . . . jest came across it by accident.'

She folded it gently, tying it round her greying hair, her fingers assured after all these years.

'Ey, Mal? What 'bout them times we ad together then, out on-a moor? Wouldn' be surprised if our David wern conceived . . .'

'Yeah . . . wish I'd-a found a condom.'

'Wha yew on about, Malcolm? It don' mean nothin t' yew, do it?'

She whipped the scarf off, flung it on top of the clothing and, turning, slammed the door shut, leaving me alone.

I'm here on the tip a week later, wondering if that couple will ever return, keeping the scarf with me for company. Again, I walk down the dip to where I saw them and birds rise, startled, behind me.

CATHERINE MERRIMAN

Aberrance in the Emotional Spectrum

At first we thought we had a problem with the COS viewer. Then with the subject under study—and this must be the case. All the same, it indicates a limitation in the equipment we haven't run across before.

For those not in psychotherapeutic or law enforcement circles, I should explain that the COS viewer is a device, still in development but already in use, capable of displaying human emotions as colours. The acronym stands for Canine Olfactory Spectrometer, though canine material hasn't actually been used since the prototype days; the name has stuck because of its descriptive power. (Most people are aware that dogs possess olfactory organs thousands of times more sensitive than their human equivalents, and that dogs can virtually 'see' smells.) The machine is constructed to ignore normally detectable odours but to pick up the tiny organic emissions associated with emotional states and reveal these through the viewer, which resembles a bulky camera. Because the machine 'sees' the emissions as coloured light, the actual organic content does not have to impact on the receptor (the associated 'light' radiation is enough) which means the device can be used not only through unobstructed air, but also through glass or other transparencies. Use of the machine requires a high level of skill—our partnership, for instance, consists of a psychologist (myself) and a behaviour analyst (my colleague Felicity)—but the benefits are huge. It has added immeasurably to our arsenal of interpretive techniques. The Derek and Felicity team has, on numerous occasions, saved lives.

One of the most fascinating findings, discovered early on in the research, is that the colours seen by us through the COS viewer bear close parallels to colours accepted linguistically across the world as being associated with particular emotions. This suggests that these colours, though invisible to the naked human eye, are nonetheless subliminally registered—possibly by our own deficient olfactory organs—and that this 'intuitive' perception has influenced language.

White or yellow, for instance, is emitted at times of fear. Of the two, white is the easier to interpret, though the harder, in our line of work, to deal with. It indicates the emotion of pure fear. We are very careful with subjects emitting bright white, as extreme fear is a stupefying emotion, and subjects emitting bright white are prone to irrationality and to sudden, often dangerously impulsive actions. They require calm handling and intense reassurance before anything more constructive can take place. Yellow, whether bright or pale, is easier to work with. Yellow, in language, is associated with cowardice, and you can see how this has arisen, but we see it as an unhelpful interpretation. In our view, yellow indicates a level and type of fear where rational thought and judgement are still operating. Where, that is, the subject can see the way ahead, but is too frightened, *just at this moment,* to take it. We can work productively on yellow.

Black is the colour of anger. (Yes, black, in the emotional spectrum, unlike in the light spectrum, is a 'colour' in its own right.) We are careful with subjects emitting black too, though our responses may be more active and dynamic. Over a variable length of time black tends to fade, like newsprint, to grey. Grey is the colour of depression, grief, sadness, hopelessness. It is actually easier to tackle black-emitters than grey-emitters, because black-emitters are more alert and more amenable to communication. Grey-emitters are frustratingly poor listeners and can be highly resistant to suggestion or advice. As Felicity puts it—and this is a statement of fact, not an unkindness—'the losers have given up'. However, as long as they remain grey, and don't suddenly flash over into black, they are usually dangers only to themselves.

Red, which is the colour of both guilt and shame (they're not the same, of course, but the viewer isn't refined enough to distinguish between them) we see only rarely. People ask if this colour is more prevalent in women than in men, because women, it is often said, are 'better' at feeling guilt, but this hasn't been our experience. I, for instance, have been known to emit bursts of red, but Felicity never! Perhaps men make up for lower levels of guilt with higher levels of shame. In any case, most of our work subjects, at the time we're viewing them, are not red-emitters. That, very often, is precisely their problem.

We are more likely, indeed, to see blue-emitters. Blue is what all of us emit when we are 'unemotional', 'relaxed' or, paradoxically, 'concentrating'—presumably because our minds, at times of concentration, are too occupied to be emotional. Blue is particularly strongly seen just before sleep, or immediately after the cessation of severe pain. It can be induced by meditative techniques. There is a yogi we have tested who emits blue almost perpetually, an amazing and rather chilling sight. The blue-emitter subjects we see at work are vaguely chilling too, because the colour indicates a mood totally inappropriate to the occasion. However blue-emitters retain full powers of intellect—many are alarmingly and deviously clever—and are usually open to argument, especially if this can be couched so as to appeal to their strong sense of self-interest.

Green can indicate envy, as it is used metaphorically in language, but, when it does, is a very yellow green. That kind of envy, we suspect, must contain an element of past, unconquered fear. It is the begrudgement of others for what one feels one could have achieved oneself, if one had been more courageous. For those who could not possibly hope to have achieved what is envied, but are still in the grip of a powerful 'envious' emotion, the colour emitted is more likely to be black. Anger, that is. There is some difference among psychologists regarding green, but personally I associate it with bitterness, and, where it veers more towards turquoise, which bright green can decay to over time, with cynicism.

The colour of happiness, it surprises most people to

learn, is not a pure, primary, jolly colour. Nor is it the colour of sunrises, or verdant pastures, or brilliant starshine. It is, in fact, brown. Indeed, all positive emotions fall somewhere in the brown range. My own view is that in true euphoria all emotional charges are released simultaneously, in a kind of ecstatic explosion, and it is this combined surge that gives us the brownish emission, as well as the inner sense of feeling gloriously 'whole'.

I have only once seen a strong brown-emitter while at work, and this subject had, until the very last minute, been one of the very rare red-emitters. He was impossible to negotiate with, because he clearly wanted the release of death—he had just killed his wife and at the time was seriously threatening his children —and he was, I would say, a deeply tortured individual. He became a brown-emitter in the last few seconds before the police shot him. He had arranged himself in a brightly lit window as a clear, easy target, and that was when the emission began. I told the marksman responsible this, and possibly it helped him in his debriefing.

Love and hate, despite being categorized in the textbooks as sentiments rather than emotions, still have colour emissions associated with them. These emissions, however, are more directional—ie, they are aimed at something—and they occur as flashes, very often, rather than as the glows of all-pervading moods. Having said that, hate, at least, seems a remarkably durable emotion; it's been our experience that hate towards a particular other may persist indefinitely, even if it is activated only for short bursts at a time; while anger, say, with which hate is often associated, seems to break down to depression (grey), bitterness (green), or some other emotion relatively quickly. The colour of hate is a deep, dark, consistent purple, one of the richest and most easily detectable colours in the emotional spectrum. The colour of love, on the other hand, is neither consistent nor uniform, suggesting that the sentiment itself is more complex. Its colour is generally a shade of warm brown (it falls, naturally, within the euphoric range) but often includes flickers of pale white (suggesting anxiety), sometimes flashes of black (fierceness, or aggression?) and sometimes a soft dove grey (pain, sadness, longing?). Sometimes, under all this 'interference' from other colours, the warm brown background is almost swamped out. We rarely see it while we're at work.

I have oversimplified the above in the interests of clarity; in real life human beings, especially highly stressed human beings, as our subjects tend to be, are often in the grip of—and thus emitting the colours of—more than one emotion, and these emotions may be conflicting. Oscillation between emotions is also common. This is why the interpretation of COS images requires great skill. But although we as operators have sometimes found ourselves defeated by the more complex colour patterns, and have had to fall back on more traditional interpretive techniques (which, when unsighted, we of course do anyway) we have always, when using the viewer, had material to work with. Up till now.

Our problem is that we now have a subject—Subject A, I'll call him—who, for significant periods (up to 43 minutes, so far) emits nothing detectable through the COS viewer at all. This is unprecedented. The only zero recordings previously encountered have been those of sleeping subjects (when not in REM phases) or of unconscious or catatonic subjects. Subject A, however, is indisputably conscious, not remotely catatonic, and yet still, from time to time, registers nothing.

At first—while we were still on site—we thought we had an intermittent fault in the viewer. Our resourceful young technician, Peter, had managed to install a receptor right inside the building, so we were able to train it on Subject A almost constantly during the negotiations, and our natural assumption when the viewer blanked was that we had a fault. The machine can't pick up anything except emotional discharge, so in its absence all you get is a fuzzy nothingness, like a television picture with the aerial disconnected. However we did notice that when the hostage was in frame we regained normal reception—brilliant white face and hands, poor lad, with a stripe down the front indicating an open shirt or jacket—and back at the station we experimented further. Subject A still had periods of non-emission, but when, during one of these, the viewer was switched to another subject (Felicity) a normal picture immediately returned. (Felicity is always willing to be guinea pig, probably because she habitually emits shades of blue, which she attributes to a naturally relaxed disposition and the absence of a punitive super-ego. It's generous of her to so often volunteer; she knows I dislike being viewed. If we're alone I'm not so reluctant, but with others, Peter, say, especially if she is giving him attention, I find it hard to suppress emissions of jealousy (green) or dislike (pale purple). It is our little joke.)

This control observation has, anyway, ruled out a glitch in the machinery. Felicity wonders if extreme psychopathy—and Subject A does exhibit profound psychopathic traits—might be the cause. Perhaps some psychopaths are capable of, quite simply, feeling nothing. I would be happier with this explanation if we had come across it before. We deal with psychopaths regularly in this job and, in my experience, while they are capable of emitting any colour except red (guilt and shame are notoriously absent from their emotional repertoire) their 'resting' colour, as it were, tends to be blue. That is, when not provoked or stimulated to other reactions, they tend to calmness. I have met several who, under the most appallingly tense circumstances, nevertheless gave all the COS appearance of being smugly at ease with themselves. (Note: the fact that Felicity is commonly a blue-emitter does not mean that she has psychopathic tendencies! In her case, being a professional, a relaxed unemotional calmness is entirely appropriate.)

Luckily we have Subject A safely in custody and since he is apparently delighted to be the focus of so much scientific attention, we hope, with his cooperation, to get to the truth. We have followed our usual work pattern: Felicity has been through the files and prepared a case study, while I have been picking up what I can from observing interviews with the released hostage and witnesses. (I know Felicity feels that occasionally these roles should be reversed, but her skills at scanning files and wordprocessing reports are far superior to mine—women seem to have a natural aptitude for keyboarding—and my observational talents, with fifteen years more clinical experience, far exceed hers. Each to their own. If push came to shove—which of course it never would—I am, in any case, by virtue of seniority, the higher ranking officer.)

I have just read Felicity's report. I've seen worse, though it still doesn't make pleasant reading. Subject A is what, in common parlance, one would call a sex maniac. His victims are young men, preferably *uniformed* young men (Felicity cleverly spotted this connection—what an eye for detail), who he invites back to his house and then is unwilling to release. He is a physically intimidating man with a controlling, gloating manner that terrifies his victims, but he is not gratuitously violent. He does not sexually assault the young men but humiliates them by satisfying himself sexually in their presence. The longest he has detained a victim (as far as we know) has been six days, after which the young man was released distressed but not seriously harmed. Since his current victim, like previous victims, accompanied him home freely, he is not being charged with kidnapping or abduction, but with ABH (this victim tried with some determination to leave and got knocked about a bit) and false imprisonment. We know a lot about Subject A because he is already on file—there have been complaints before, though none, due to the reluctance of victims to press charges, came to anything—and because the man himself is being remarkably cooperative in interview. According to my own researches, the young man we released today met Subject A two nights ago in a club where the clientele dress up in outrageous 'fancy dress' outfits. The victim was wearing a uniform (of a tasteless stormtrooper type) and for this reason attracted Subject A's attention. Luckily the young man was with friends before he was persuaded to depart with Subject A, and these friends not only reported him missing the next day, but could also give us a very accurate description of the man he had left with. In all fairness I should say that these friends come across as entirely normal individuals, living very ordinary, respectable, daytime lives. The young victim himself is a hospital nurse. Twenty years ago, when I was their age, any desire to dress up in flagrantly kinky clothes—whatever one's sexual orientation—would have been satisfied behind drawn domestic curtains, not paraded in public places. I made this observation to Felicity, and she retorted that lack of guilt or shame about such things are healthy developments and make the world a much safer place. I bow to her opinion. For the young man in question, given that the speed of his release was entirely due to the unembarrassed frankness of his friends, she must certainly be right.

Thinking about this has made me realize that we have never before dealt with a serious sex offender. As negotiators and interpreters Felicity and I deal with a range of individuals, but our commonest subjects are aggrieved, desperate husbands or partners, and holed-up villains. I cannot recall attending a single past siege involving a sex offender who was using his victim as hostage. (Which is not to say that hostages are not now and again sexually assaulted by their captors, but there is a difference.) I can also not recall a case before where the captor has treated the incident—even before apprehension and arrest—with such levity, almost as if he were enjoying it. Perhaps he was, though the COS viewer rarely displayed brown hues. Instead, at those times when Subject A, viewed with the naked eye or through a camera, appeared closest to showing pleasure, it simply went blank.

We have now sent Subject A upstairs to the FME to be medically examined and to have samples of his blood and urine taken. (We are considering the possibility that he has some physical peculiarity or biochemical imbalance that blocks certain emissions.) In the meantime Felicity and I are taking a long-overdue break in the staff canteen. This break would be more enjoyable if Peter hadn't joined us—he has an annoying habit of calling Felicity 'Fliss', and is in my opinion presumptuously over-familiar with her. Felicity does not encourage him but nor does she slap him down, which really she would be wise to; this station takes a dim view of male-female friendships across ranks. However I know she would be sharp with me if I remonstrated with him on her behalf—she is a very modern woman—so I have to pretend to ignore him. One of the things we have been discussing, very much not for the first time, is how much easier our task would be if COS readings could be recorded. The fact that they can't be is why each COS operation requires the attendance of two interpreters, since it is unreasonable to expect one person to be permanently glued to the eyepiece. Not that I'd be without Felicity, of course, but neither of us comes cheap. The chance to rerun observations, too, would be enormously helpful. In this case, for instance, having established that the 'visual silences' were not due to machine error, we could have rerun all the episodes, and perhaps spotted common precipitating factors. However, although the time will soon come—all that's needed, Peter says, is a device to transform the signals into ones that register on magnetic tape—it has not arrived yet. Notes and memory are all very well, but neither can record everything.

We have been invited up to have a word with the FME, who has completed his examination. Subject A is now back in the cells. Peter wanted to come too but I discouraged him—interpretation is not a technician's business—and he took the hint. The FME says Subject A is a healthy, normal 38 year old in all physical respects that he can determine, though of course we will have to wait for the blood and urine analysis to confirm this. He does however have one very interesting observation to make. Subject A, he says, gives all the appearance of being in a state of permanent sexual arousal. Body flush, pupil enlargement, the lot. The taking of a urine sample, he says, was anything but the quick, simple procedure it usually is. He is a clever man, the FME, and before examining Subject A had done his homework by reading Felicity's case notes. It is his opinion that it was the presence of the escort constable that was exciting Subject A (because his state of arousal visibly heightened when the officer was in view) and he suggests that Subject A is finding the whole situation, the whole experience of being surrounded by men in uniforms (as one is, both in a siege situation and in a police station) intensely gratifying.

There is an obvious conclusion to be drawn from this. It surprises me; I had somehow imagined that in a state of acute arousal the emotions would be very forceful. And, as emissions, strongly, powerfully brown—the culmination of acute arousal, orgasm, is surely the ultimate in euphoria. But perhaps, if you view the state as an inward-turned, self-centred, black-hole sort of event, one that sucks in, rather then emits outward . . . the words *consumed with lust* suggest themselves . . . or, indeed, see orgasm as a release of a quite different order to emotional release, involving experience and feeling quite beyond the normal range . . .

My goodness. The ramifications could be stupendous. My brain is jumping with possibilities. But first things first. We must, absolutely must, attempt to repeat the observation. As soon as possible. And not with Subject A—that would prove nothing.

I wonder if Peter would help. Felicity has returned to the canteen to tell him about the doctor's findings. It's not something you could properly ask of an outsider, but Peter would see a request in the right light, surely, since he has shown himself just as keen as us to investigate the anomaly. I'm sure I haven't seen anything about orgasmic COS emissions, or lack of them, in the literature. Preliminary results, even based on a very ad hoc experiment, would be of great interest to a lot of people—not just COS interpreters. I can see an article in it already. Perhaps several. And how difficult would it be to arrange? We could do it here. Peter and a few rude magazines in Interview 6 (the room with the one-way glass) and me with the COS viewer next door. If I promised to keep my eyes on the viewer eyepiece until it was over, it would even be relatively unembarrassing, since he wouldn't have to face the viewer and, if we were proved right, would actually disappear for the crucial moments.

On the other hand, in his shoes, I wouldn't do it. But this may just be because I couldn't contemplate either Peter or Felicity in the next room. Felicity because she is a woman; and Peter because, frankly, I don't trust him. It's not that I think he'd actually do anything improper (what, short of inviting his friends in, could count as 'improper?) but I do think that these sort of experiments have to be conducted in an atmosphere of trust. These sorts of experiments especially. Otherwise, among other things, one can imagine performance difficulties. But I doubt lack of trust would be a problem for Peter. We may not be bosom buddies, but I'm sure he has never doubted my professionalism.

It is a great shame that COS pictures can't be recorded. I had a kind of flash fantasy then, of myself and Felicity, alone in a room with a recording viewer . . .

And that disgraceful thought raises an further point. I wonder, if men's emotional side really is put on hold, swamped out, or perhaps implodes, at times of intense lustfulness or arousal, the same is true for women? This question will doubtless have already occurred to Felicity—she is very hot on the female perspective. On the other hand it's not a question we could investigate immediately, as we would need to draft in a fully briefed female volunteer, since Felicity, for propriety's sake, would have to man (or rather woman!) the viewer. But we could settle the male question straight away. I think, while my enthusiasm is high, and we are all still on the premises, I will find Felicity and discuss it with her.

We have had a long talk. I am not at all—*at all*—happy with the outcome, in fact I am deeply *un*happy. However I know that if I refuse to go along with what Felicity proposes she will take umbrage, and probably accuse me of questioning her professionalism. She has already suggested that my reluctance is bound up with my personal feelings towards her, which I automatically denied, though of course she is right. Her argument is that, if we do as she proposes, we will kill two birds with one stone, as it were, need to involve no one outside the team, and will obtain the results we want (hopefully) very fast. The only counter arguments I have actually articulated are that a) her way is bound to be very much more indecorous and embarrassing for the participants, and b) that all research shows that women can bring themselves to orgasm very much faster through masturbation than in the act of intercourse. To the first she scoffed, 'Really, Derek, we're scientists, embarrassment doesn't come into it,' and to the second she replied, 'So what?' She went on to point out that while a man might be able to set the ball rolling with dirty magazines, the same was not true for women (or for herself, anyway) and that the attentions of an attractive male, with whom she already has a bond of friendship and trust, would be much more likely to achieve results. And then she said, 'It's not as if the whole world will be watching, Derek. Only you.'

A small crumb of comfort in all this is that Peter apparently also took some persuading. He goes up, marginally, in my estimation. He has agreed only after reminders that COS images are grossly undefined, compared to camera images, that, if the experiment goes as we expect, they will both be invisible to me for at least some of the time (as long as I keep my eyes on the viewer eyepiece) and, of course, that the images are unrecordable. I have a strong suspicion that both Peter and I are being bullied into agreement by a spurious logic employed for dubious ends, but those ends will achieve ours too, and so, despite our—or at least my—deep reservations, Felicity has got her way.

They have removed the table from the interview room and borrowed a clean mattress from the rape suite storeroom (there has to be irony in that) which they have laid out on the floor. I have lined up the COS viewer next door and tested it through the glass. Peter is currently emitting yellows and whites, interspersed with bursts of brown, ie he is oscillating between acute anxiety and anticipation, while Felicity is emitting her usual blue, with occasional flashes of rich brown. These seem particularly strong when her body—and so possibly her gaze—turns to the one-way glass, which I find vaguely disconcerting.

The deed is done. It's a good thing I haven't had a COS viewer trained on me. I imagine the results would have been a whirling kaleidoscope of colours, none of them remotely brown. Greens and blacks, I suspect, in the main. Flashes of purple, too, very possibly, as the experiment progressed.

Felicity, at the start, lost her brown flashes and became exclusively blue. Concentrating on reassuring Peter, I guessed. He slowly lost his whites and yellows, and by the time he was naked (you can't see the clothes, of course, but you can see the emergence of coloured flesh) he had become consistently brown. Then more of Felicity became visible—turning brown too—and their shapes became excruciatingly active. I haven't watched naked bodies through the machine since the very early development days, and—obviously, otherwise we wouldn't be doing this—never bodies preparing for sexual intercourse. The images are quite defined enough to stir intense feelings of voyeurism—at several points I had to force myself not to pull away from the eyepiece. But then, just as I was wondering how much more I could possibly take, Felicity's glowing brown shape simply faded away. This should have caused a surge of brown emissions from me, given what we had set out to prove, but I am absolutely sure didn't. Indeed, I clicked on the 'Felicity' stop watch with such violence I'm surprised I didn't damage it. Peter remained visible for only a few seconds before he too vanished. I clicked the second stopwatch. I don't know which was worse, being able to see them, or not being able to. I remained watching what appeared to be a blank screen for some considerable time (which additionally enraged me—there was no need for them to spin it out) before Peter reappeared (I clicked his watch off) followed a minute or so later by Felicity (hers off too). Felicity emerged a deep rich blue, interspersed with pulses of pale brown, while Peter was a uniform warm rich brown, which, over the time I continued to watch them, showed no sign of fading. I fear he may be a sentimentalist, the silly man.

I removed my eyes from the viewer once I was sure they were dressed and upright. Felicity, through the one-way glass, looked her usual neat business-like self, though, in my opinion, suspiciously bright-eyed, while Peter looked idiotically tousled and sheepish. In a moment of spite I toyed with the idea of reporting that no visual silences had occurred at all, but decided that the implications of this would dismay Peter far more than Felicity, who would probably just find it funny. And the lie would be bound to be exposed at a later date, since we're not the only people using these machines. Anyway, look at what we had just proved—hardly the moment to consider professional suicide.

However, I do not think I can continue to work with a woman like Felicity. I had no idea—really, not an inkling—that she disliked me so much. 'All in the name of science, Derek,' she has just said to me, her voice so offhand and airy that I felt a powerful urge to strangle her. Does she think I'm stupid? Does she think I can't see through her? No; the answer, of course, is that she knows exactly how obvious her motives are to me—I am, after all, a highly skilled interpreter—but simply doesn't care. The manipulative cleverness of the blue-emitter. Two birds with one stone, as she said before we started: she has punished me (for whatever crimes I have apparently committed) and indulged her lust for Peter; and yet remains herself, entirely—and in the eyes of the world, even courageously—above reproach. I shall definitely request a transfer. My eyes are now truly open. The woman is a menace to her colleagues. What a tramp.

Delivery

A decade or more back, Harry had seen off Social Services with his axe. The two women had called at the cottage, ignored all his shouts to go away, and had left only when, finally, he snatched open the front door. With the axe in his hand. Not lifted threateningly; merely hanging, head down, from his slack right arm. But it had done the trick; they left, and never returned.

Harry kept the axe in the hallway after that, when it was not in use. Though uses were frequent; axes were versatile tools. With it he smashed up the wooden pallets that his next door neighbour left outside his gate, shattering the soft wood to kindling, which, when the evenings became dark and cold, he burnt in his small grate. (His nephew said he should thank the neighbour for his generosity. Why? Harry thought. The man owned a builder's yard down in the village, the pallets cost him nothing; he was merely disposing of them for free.)

He also used the axe as a hammer. Harry often nailed things. The nails came free with the pallets, either bursting from the grain as he smashed them up, or collecting in the bottom of the firegrate after the wood had burnt away. He used the nails, and strips of wood from the pallets, to board up the back door. Tapped the heads in with the flat side of the axe head. How could you guard two doors, at opposite sides of the house? And all that draught.

Once—Harry admitted he had been feeling very distant that day, very locked in the past—he had nailed his own hand to the kitchen table. He had solved the problem of holding the nail upright, ready for the blow, by laying his hand on the surface palm upwards, and steadying the nail in curled-over fingers. The funny thing was that, at the same time as he was lining up the impaling stroke, he had been frightened of missing, and directly striking his flesh. But his aim had been true. The nail embedded itself deeply enough to make a spike under the wooden table top. There had been very little blood. Only a brief shock of pain. The briefness had disconcerted him. However, for the half day he sat immobilised on the kitchen chair before releasing himself with an underarm, under-table swing of the axe, he had felt temporarily relieved. Temporarily restored. Once freed, he had worked the nail from his flesh under the ice-cold winter tap water, and his hand now bore only the tiniest of scars.

Today, when rapping on the front door summoned him, the axe was in its usual place, propped below the row of wall nails that acted as coat pegs. But today Harry opened the door without checking first, because it was a Sunday—he had heard the village church bells not an hour ago—and knew it would be his nephew, Joe, with the groceries. He swung the door open and moved forward to block the threshold with his body, as he always did. Even Joe couldn't be relied on not to try to carry the box inside.

'Here you are then, Harry.' Joe grinned at him, a foolish, ingratiating grin. His nephew, Harry thought, had been an ugly pug of a young man, and now, in middle age, was a physical disgrace. Did some soft factory job that had left cushions of idleness around his waist. At his age, Harry had been hard as a nut. Strong as the steel he worked with.

'And,' said Joe, stepping to one side, revealing another figure behind the box he was holding, 'this is my boy, Neil. Now Harry—'

Harry grasped the box, interrupting him. He tried to back into the hall.

'No,' said Joe, still smiling, but firmly now. He put a steadying hand on the open door. 'You listen a minute, Harry. You remember what I told you last week?'

Over the top of the cardboard box Harry stared at the boy Neil. The panic subsided. He was a boy. As tall as his father, but slim as a whip. Blonde hair tucked behind his ears. Something glinted on an earlobe. An earring? Jewellery? But he was, undoubtedly, a boy. His nephew's son. Since he had never seen him before, he had to take this on trust.

'D'you remember, Harry? I warned you last week. I'll be working Sundays up to Christmas now. Just brought Neil round so it doesn't surprise you, like. Next Sunday he'll bring the stuff. Got his driving test a month ago, clever lad. It'll be same as usual. Only him, not me. OK?'

'Hello, Mr Daniels.' The boy's eyelashes batted like a girl's. 'It'll be a pleasure.'

'He's your uncle,' Joe chided him. 'Not Mr Daniels. It's your great uncle Harry.'

Harry wanted to say something, but it was days since he had last spoken out loud and his throat muscles took a while to respond. Before he had made more than a creaking noise Joe tapped the box and said, 'Two dozen candles in there, in case you're low. You'll be needing them, now the hour's changed. Slow burners, guaranteed. You tell Neil, now, if there's anything special you want for next week.'

Harry shook his head. He didn't want anyone here instead of Joe. Certainly not that boy. He had a face that had escaped from somewhere.

He closed the door against Joe's feet and carried the box into the living room. After a minute he heard car doors slam, an engine fire and fade. They had gone.

His mind thudded. Was it a trick? After all these years, were they trying to catch him out? His hands shook, unpacking the box. As usual he tossed the apples to one side. What use were apples to a man? The boy's face flashed vivid in his mind. Just like Lizzie. Had they known? Waited all these years, knowing the boy would one day look right, and then brought him to the cottage, trailed him like a lure. Had he reacted? Betrayed anything? He couldn't picture himself. Couldn't remember.

All afternoon and evening his thoughts raced. In the candlelight their destinations darkened; the corners of the room guttered with the most patient, devious revenges. Was this why her family had kept him alive, all these years? His own brothers had given up on him decades ago. What thanks had he ever given them? What did they get out of it? How innocent, how stupid of him. He had never considered motives.

Late evening he heated up a can of Chunky Vegetable soup on his camping stove and spooned it down with half a packet of digestive biscuits. He had been cold earlier, he realized. But afterwards, though he was less chilled, he still felt threatened enough to nail up the front door. Just with a pallet plank, and six warped, charcoal-blackened nails. It was the act of doing it, really. It wouldn't take a moment to prise off next time he wanted to go outside.

All week, as he pottered through the dark, mildew-stained rooms, he dreamed. The dreams lurched to and fro in time. Snippets of his past. He remembered how, even at the beginning, just after Lizzie's death, her family had rallied to him. How their men had stood, stiff and protective, around him at the funeral. No; you'd expect that, wouldn't you? Not strange at all. She was one of them. Of course they'd grieved for her too. Joe had been a child then, no more than ten or twelve, puffed up and red faced, because he was black-suited with the men, not behind curtains with the women.

And perhaps in the five years afterwards, while he was still working, contact would have been natural. Joe's father, her brother, God rest his soul, had been a crane driver at the steel works. Of course they exchanged words, nods. Nothing suspicious in that.

But afterwards? When he stopped going to work? When the retreat he hadn't realized possible, until any alternative became impossible, came suddenly upon him? As if a cloak of numbness had lifted, exposing a nakedness of raw, flinching, appalled flesh. Why, then, had they followed him here? Sought him out, tried to cajole him into the world again, and, when that failed, kept tabs on him, took over responsibility for his survival. They held his invalidity book. Now his pension book. Paid his bills, few as they were. Just water, these days, and some new property tax. Shopped for him, food and occasional clothes, brought boxes round weekly. Why? And why for so long? Even after her brother died, when there was no one left who could truly remember her, why?

Because he dozed frequently during the day, he was awake for long periods at night. When the grate had burnt to cold white ash and only the faint haze of the nightlight candle near the door relieved the blackness, his thoughts became more fantastic. He saw the family in a huddle, heads together, whispering. A cabal, planning, plotting. Thinking long-term. Perhaps the boy wasn't one of them at all, but someone searched for over the years. An actor, specially chosen. Or—the limits dissolved in the dark—even manufactured. Blueprinted, put together, moulded by them, over many years, in her likeness.

In daylight his thoughts were easier to order, and of lesser scope. He wondered, at one point, if they simply wanted the cottage. Perhaps they thought that, by showing him the boy, they could scare him to death. Thought they'd earned his property. But they wouldn't get it. He had made no will; his own relatives, not hers, would inherit. And they must know this. Everyone understood inheritance.

So, if it was a confession they wanted from him, they would have to try harder. Shock couldn't do it. They would have to be more inventive, more cunning than that. He had seen through their plot.

By Sunday morning he had almost convinced himself that, when the door banged later, it would be Joe as usual behind it. That the boy had been a one-off, a tactic that, having failed, they wouldn't try again.

He heard the church bells, and padded expectantly round the house. After a while it came to him that Joe was late. Perhaps that was it . . . last week had been his final visit. He had brought the boy with him to show him why. After twenty five years of keeping him alive, they were now abandoning him. They had grown bored with their game.

Then the door rattled. Harry strode to the hall, slipped the blade of the axe under the plank of wood, frowning at it—had he really not been out for seven days?—and prised it off. He propped the axe against the wall again and opened the door.

'Sorry I'm a bit late, Mr Daniels.' The boy's head was tilted almost to his shoulder in apology. 'Hope you haven't been worrying. I was out last night. Headache like a pile-driver this morning.' He smiled radiantly down into the box he was holding. 'But it's all here.'

Harry didn't take the box off him immediately. He wanted another look at the boy's face, while he was trapped in front of him. Lizzie had been older, of course. But the same golden hair. The same pale, angelic complexion. The same incongruously dark, long eyelashes. Indecently long, on a boy. And the same radiant smile. But what had the boy said? Something about headaches. Aha, aha. He felt clever, to have spotted the reference. That clinched it. Aches and pains. Headaches, bellyaches. She must have told them, all those years ago. They must have passed it down, one generation to the next.

He found his arms reaching out for the box; which was a mistake, because it suddenly came to him that the boy should be inside the cottage. That inside was where he belonged. Where he had escaped from. Now it was too late. As he took the weight his throat grumbled but, without words in his head, he could form nothing aloud.

'D'you want anything special for next week, Mr Daniels? You only got to say. And Mam says do you need any more blankets, now it's getting colder?'

Harry started to shake his head, as he always did, but then caught himself. No. That was it. Load the boy up. It would provide an excuse. He nodded curtly.

'More blankets? Yes?' The boy's eyes urged him to confirm it.

'Hmm.' He nodded again, more emphatically.

The boy looked delighted. Proud he had forced a response.

'That's fine, Mr Daniels. I won't forget. See you next week then.' And he waved, actually waved, as he walked back to Joe's car.

Harry banged the door shut with his knee. As he thumped the box on to the cottage table he felt cross with himself. A missed opportunity. A whole week to wait. He unloaded the box and, throwing the apples aside, found himself transferring the anger. Headaches and bellyaches. Always headaches and bellyaches. Not in the early days, of course, when he'd taken her out on his arm, oh no. Then she had flashed like a beacon, batted those lashes, bestowed that radiance. Flattering, when they were courting. A woman, as young and beautiful as she; made him feel a prince. But afterwards, when she was a married woman, it hadn't been seemly. A seemly woman, a woman he could trust, he would have allowed her freedom. A seemly woman could have had friends, as many as she wished, could have come and gone as she pleased. But could she understand this? She could not. Instead of moderating her behaviour, she had sulked. Sulked and complained. Headaches and bellyaches. When he wanted to touch her. Or when she wanted to escape from him. Visiting the doctor. How could he say no to her seeing the doctor? Except that there was never anything wrong. Excuses, excuses. Visiting her mother, or a friend, more like; or strolling the town. He'd caught her in a lie several times. There were rights and duties in marriage. No one could say he hadn't been a good husband, no one: a mature man, with a steady, well-paid job, even a house of his own. He'd been tolerant, and self-controlled. Some men hit their misbehaving wives. Not he. Not once. Never. He had loved her. Even told her so—not kept it to himself, like so many husbands. But you had to be firm. Had to set boundaries. Force boundaries on them, if necessary.

A sense of outrage built in him overnight. He hardly slept. How dare, how dare, her family stir him up again like this. And as he pushed the anger on to them, he felt it slip from her. Dear Lizzie. She was as she was. She'd given him four years of joy, while they courted. More than a year of pride and contentment, when they were first married. Then two years of frustration and disappointment, and then her death. On balance, in shortened form, probably much like any other marriage. Ups and down, but the good outweighing the bad. All marriages ended in acrimony, or death.

The next day he went upstairs, the first time in many months. Across the stairwell spiders had slung dusty hammocks that stretched and collapsed to dirty string as he walked through them. He went into the bedroom where the double bedstead, unslept in for thirty years, still stood in the middle of the room. The bare mattress was velvety with dust. He opened the wardrobe and touched her dresses. Silly styles. He had loved the full, fussy, petticoated frocks the girls wore in his own youth; these that had followed were skimpy, shapeless things. Bold colours, bold designs, but not womanly. They had been hers, though, and she had still looked beautiful in them.

He removed his favourite, a blue sleeveless dress with white piping round the armholes and neck that she had thought dull, but he thought made her look like a blonde Jackie Kennedy. Or Princess Grace. All the posh women had them. He carried the dress downstairs on its hanger, hammered a nail into a beam near the window with the back of the axe, and hung the dress from it, so he could sit in front of the evening fire and still see it. It upset him, especially when it swayed as he brushed past, but it was a reminder. He didn't want the feelings to fade before next Sunday.

Over the days, he tidied up a little. If he was to have a visitor, and such a special visitor, he didn't want to give the impression of having lost his grip. He didn't want to be pitied. He could do nothing about the mildew on the walls, the stains on the carpet around the camping stove, but he could clear the floor, put old tins and packets into cardboard boxes, stack them against the wall. There was no shortage of boxes. He spread old blankets across the chairs to cover the holes. Why not? The boy was bringing new ones.

He found eating difficult as the time drew near. There

was a sticky, metallic taste in his mouth that no amount of tea or soup could wash away. A pressure seemed to be building in his head which made his thoughts distant, as if they were being squeezed through a narrow, constricted space. Rather like that time he had nailed himself to the table; only this time he didn't want the relief of that. When the sensation became intense he went outside and broke up pallets. The exercise was distracting.

On the Sunday he waited for the church bells and, as they rang, felt the chimes jangle inside his empty belly. He forced himself to eat two tablespoonfuls of sugar, straight from the bag, for his lunch. You had to keep your energy up.

He practised using his voice. Cleared his throat, coughed, to make sure his airways were clear. Said his own name, Harry. Easy. Harry. Harry. Then Joe. The 'o' noise pulled unnaturally at his lower jaw. Jo-o. Then Lizzie. Just a flick of the tongue. A hum in his throat. Lizzie. Like a saw buzzing. And finally Neil. Neil. The word sounded like an order. A natural, authoritative sound. Neil. His voice, saying it, gained confidence and strength.

He was listening out today and heard the car draw up out on the lane. He went to stand in the hallway. The knock was more a scrape; the boy must have his hands full. He opened the door. There was a pile of blankets over the boy's shoulder and his arms were wide with box.

'Here you are then, Mr Daniels.' That smile flashed at him again. 'Blankets too. Told you I wouldn't forget.'

Harry nodded at him and, though it took huge effort, breaking the habit of thirty years, stepped aside.

'Oh right. Take them in, shall I?' The boy looked surprised, but pleased.

Harry nodded again and, as the boy passed with his load, reached down his right leg for the wooden handle of the axe. He made a grunting noise when the boy tried to go the wrong way, into the back kitchen, and the boy glanced behind him and obeyed the jerk of his head by turning into the living room.

'Ooh, Mr Daniels, it's cold in here.' Neil humped the box on to the table. He slid the blankets from his shoulder on to the back of one of the chairs. Then stared around. His lips pursed and a small line creased the skin between his eyebrows. 'You managing all right, Mr Daniels?' His voice had become faint, as if it was hard to speak and look at the same time. 'Oh, Mr Daniels. I don't need to rush off. Can I do anything for you?'

Harry knew he did want the boy to do something, or to do something with the boy, but couldn't remember what. He was mesmerized by the boy's appearance. So fresh and pure, standing there in his grey sweatshirt with a hood at the back, his blue jeans. And his face: the beauty of his profile, the sweep of his silky hair, the glint of gold at his ear. The boy's eyes had reached the window and halted, resting on the hanging dress. His lips parted, but he said nothing.

'Lizzie,' Harry said. The blue material reminded him. That was why the boy was here, because of Lizzie.

'Is he what?' The boy pulled his eyes from the dress. He looked puzzled, but eager to understand.

'Lizzie,' said Harry again.

'Oh, *Lizzie*. Sorry, Mr Daniels. Who's Lizzie?'

The boy was a good actor. *Who's Lizzie.* Harry thought he was going to choke. But the anger cleared his mind. That was why he had brought the boy inside, to show him he knew. To expose their machinations, their conspiracy. He realized, suddenly, the purpose of the dress. The boy was their tool, their weapon. He dared to impersonate Lizzie. Well, let him do it properly. That would show them.

'Put it on,' he said.

'I'm sorry?' The boy peered at him, at a loss.

'The frock,' he said. 'Put it on.'

The boy pulled back, half laughed. 'Oh, Mr Daniels, I don't think it would suit me, do you?' His mouth dipped in and out of a smile.

'Put it on,' Harry repeated, and took a step towards him. He lifted his arm, just an inch or two.

The boy noticed the axe for the first time. His eyes

widened, darted sideways. 'I think I have to go now, Mr Daniels,' he murmured, his body shifting. 'I'll leave you in peace.'

Harry stared at him. The boy tucked his chin into his chest and walked past him, making for the doorway. The moment his back was fully turned Harry swung the axe upright, the blunt side of the head foremost, and hit him with it between the shoulder blades.

The boy staggered, made a noise like someone blowing a pea-less whistle, and dropped to his knees. Then tipped forward on to his hands. Harry walked over to the hanging dress, yanked it down, and tossed it across the boy's back.

'Put it on.'

The boy didn't respond. Harry moved round to his head, to stand between him and the doorway. The boy's golden hair was hanging forward, hiding his face. A weakling, to fall like that. He hadn't used a fraction of his full strength.

Slowly the boy lifted his head. His complexion was white, his eyelashes fluttering. 'Mr Daniels,' he whispered. 'Jesus . . . Please . . .'

Harry prodded the boy's shoulder with the head of the axe. Then pushed, hard, forcing him back on his heels. The boy's hands scrabbled at the axe, so he snatched it back again.

'Mr Daniels.' The boy's voice was shaking. 'I'm Neil. You know, Dad's . . . Joe's son . . .'

Harry swung the axe backwards, underarm, and let its own weight carry it back. The head hit the front of the boy's knee.

'Jesus Christ!' This time the boy shot upright, back into the room, staggering and stumbling, grabbing at his leg. He came to rest leaning against the back of one of the blanket-covered arm chairs. Harry scooped up the dress and threw it at him. It landed on the chair back, only inches from the boy's hands. But still he didn't take it. Harry stepped forward and lifted the axe again.

The boy glanced quickly back at him, and seemed to

go into a frenzy. He wrenched at his sweatshirt, snatching it off over his head. He was wearing a T shirt underneath, with words on it that made no sense to Harry; he ripped this off too. He fumbled with the zip at the back of the dress, pulling at the tag, again and again, shaking his head.

'I can't . . . Mr Daniels, I can't, please, it's stuck.'

'Put it on.'

The boy's face screwed up. He started to cry. Thin muscles jerked under the white skin of his torso as he wept, struggling with the zip. He twisted towards the window for more light, and Harry saw the livid mark on his back, a dent rather than a swelling, stippled with darker dots, like a freckled hen's egg.

The zip gave. Harry heard the ratchet hiss of the teeth opening. Now the boy didn't know what to do, how to put a dress on. He raised it, lowered it again, flapped it helplessly. Then, with a sob, kicked his shoes off—ugly, clumsy, sports shoes—undid his belt, and wrestled off his jeans. He was wearing bright red underpants beneath, very brief and tight, like women's panties. He stepped into the dress, swivelled it around him, and tugged it up over his narrow hips. He pushed his arms through the armholes and pulled the front up. Then stood motionless, his head bowed, forearms resting on the chair, his bare back towards Harry.

'Do it up,' Harry said.

The boy nodded, without turning. His hands crept behind his back, over his hips, fingers searching for the zip. The material was rucked inside itself; even when he found the tag he had difficulty moving it. A little way above his waist he gave up.

'I can't do it,' he whispered. He was standing so still he seemed to be vibrating.

Harry walked over to him, pulled the rucks out of the material, and tugged the zip up. The freckled bruise disappeared beneath the blue material. At the top he had to touch the boy's hair, lifting it out of the way. It was soft and fine and smelt of soap. He remembered doing this for Lizzie. Under his fingers the boy's skin shivered. He stepped back.

'Turn round,' he said, and heard his voice gruff and thick.

The boy turned. The dress gave him a waist. It was short, shorter than it had been on Lizzie, reaching only half-way down his thighs. His naked arms were white and slender, though their shape was more sculpted, more muscular than hers. The boy stood awkwardly, his weight resting on his uninjured leg. He lifted his head, blinked his long, wet eyelashes, and stared off somewhere into the corner of the room.

'Mr Daniels,' he said in a very small voice. 'Please don't touch me. Please let me go.'

The boy was mimicking her. Even in defeat. Even now their game was exposed. Her voice, her words. Next he would be saying he had a pain in his belly.

The boy gave a small cough and winced. 'I don't feel very well, Mr Daniels. I think you've hurt me.' He coughed again and a spot of bright red froth appeared at the corner of his mouth. He touched the side of his hand to it, and then stared at the hand.

Lizzie had not bled from the mouth. She had not bled from anywhere visible. Not even from her woman's parts, though the doctors said this was unusual. She had vomited, at some time during the evening, but not bled. All her split blood had stayed inside her, formed that cruel, grotesque swelling in her abdomen. But earlier, when he had been with her, there had been nothing to see. Just the sweat on her skin, which he had put down to the summer heat, and her temper. And the pain, which he had not believed.

The boy tried to say something else, but coughed instead. He had to steady himself on the chair. White face, bright cherry lips.

She had been extraordinarily white. When he had unlocked the bedroom door, after she had been quiet for a couple of hours, that was the first thing that struck him. How white she had become. Then he had smelt, and seen, the vomit on the floor under the window, and then he had failed to rouse her.

The boy's legs were buckling; he was going to fall. Harry let the axe drop and stepped forward to grasp him by the upper arms. The boy moaned and his shoulders convulsed, trying to pull away. Maybe the grip hurt him. As gently as he could Harry lowered him to the floor. He laid him on his back, straightened his limbs. The boy's body was rigid, but unresisting. Harry reached for one of the new blankets, shook it out, and spread it over him.

If he had realized she was ill, he could have saved her. If he had believed her, he could have saved her. A few hours, they said, would have made all the difference. *It's like a nail going through me, Harry* she had screamed. *Like a nail. I have to see the doctor.* And he had ignored her, because he'd heard it all before. He had locked the bedroom door on her, gone downstairs, and turned the television on, so her voice was just a distant wail in the lulls.

This was the test. Harry suddenly realized it. The knowledge shocked him, but there was no doubt about it. Joe was a cruel, ruthless man. Prepared to risk his son's life, to avenge his aunt's. Poor Neil. Poor Lizzie. Stiffly he knelt down and touched the boy's face, which was cool under his fingertips. The boy's eyelashes lifted, then closed tight again. He was trembling, his breathing shallow, but perhaps more afraid than hurt. He was just bleeding, a little, in his lungs. The sight of his own blood, perhaps, had frightened him. The blow on his back must have been harder than he'd intended, must have broken something. A rib, maybe. A sharp, puncturing rib. Harry had seen such things before, at the steel works.

And he knew what to do. He remembered what to do. The boy shouldn't be lying down. If there was blood in his lungs, he could drown in it. He must sit up. He worked an arm under the boy's shoulders, ignored the shuddering, the shrinking away, and lifted his upper body. Propped him against the chair back. Wedged him in place with blankets.

There. He sat back on his heels. He felt huge pity for the boy. Anger on his behalf. Joe had used his son. He had been lucky enough to have a son, and did not value him. Saw him only as bait. If he, Harry, had had a son—a son or daughter—he would have valued the child. His child, the doctors said, had been only the size of a tadpole when it burst out of its faulty resting place, its tiny constricting tube, killing itself, and mortally wounding its mother. A tadpole. Only eight weeks old. They hadn't even known she was pregnant.

He patted the boy's cheek again—Lizzie's cheek, he thought, the same flesh, the same essence—and grunted, 'It's all right. You'll be all right.' The boy whimpered and turned his face away, pushing it into the greasy filth of the chair back. Harry reached for the axe and leant on the handle to lever himself upright. 'Next door,' he said. 'A telephone. Don't worry.'

He left the room, and then the cottage. He opened the gate, and stepped out on to the lane. There was a breeze, blowing fresh dampness into his face. Across the small dividing field he could see his neighbour's wife already, at the side of the bungalow, her rubber-booted foot pressing a fork into the dark earth of their vegetable patch. He walked towards her, practising sounds in his head, shaping the words they would make. And, as he did so, felt a deep, triumphant sense of pride. He would pass the test. Words, from him to her, in time to save a precious life.

Robert Nisbet

Jam Jars of Seaweed and Dreams of Love

I met Martha just at a time when I was going right out of my way *to* meet somebody, one summer holiday in 1958, when Gus and I had taken the tent down to the Haven for just over a fortnight with the deliberate intention of meeting somebody, and of having the love affairs of our lifetimes. Anyway, the thing was that we got entangled with a crowd of Swansea boys, including, in particular, one hulking great pansy footballer of bronzed physique, called Dev, and in the end we got around to hating Dev's guts so much that long before the fortnight was up I had forgotten any randy impulses I'd taken with me to the Haven and was talking to Gus of spiritual elopements, wanting to succeed with Martha just to spite Dev.

By 'the Haven' anyway, I mean two tiny villages, Little Haven and Broad Haven, on St Bride's Bay, on the Pembrokeshire coast, and you may well not have heard of them. I reckon they're commercialised by now, but it wasn't too bad in 1958: there were a few people coming down from the Swansea and Cardiff areas for holidays, a few fields with caravans and tents, a weekly hop in the church hall, the odd camp-fire and groups of teenagers hanging around the chip-shop and the small café in the evenings.

This was the big attraction, of course. We were just about to go into the Sixth Form, sixteen and shaving, and now that we could go on holiday without our parents, we were all for going where the girls were. We dug out our scruffy old R.A.F. surplus tent, stuck it in Gus's old man's car and cycled down to the Haven. 'You wait, boy,' said Gus. 'There'll be some really nice girls down there.'

I suppose we could have done the job thoroughly and gone to Butlin's—a couple of the boys had—but, when it came to it, we liked the Haven. We'd been cycling down there for years, and when we were kids we used to get down there early on Saturday mornings in the summer term and fish around in the rock-pools for little creatures, anemones, starfish, small crabs, little worms, and sea-beasts we never bothered about finding out the names of. We'd collect these creatures, gather them in with seaweed of every kind, and put little clusters of them in jam jars to take home. Sometimes I'd concentrate on seaweeds only, pink and brown and every shade of green. They'd grow, too. Put in a small pebble or two and the moss and the weed will grow on it, and the water will darken and grow rich. Then we'd worry that the creatures would die and would take the jars back to the Haven and empty them back into the pools. We were no biologists, but we did enjoy collecting those sea creatures. So, even when we went down that summer, we took a supply of jars along.

The first evening, though, all our plans were aimed at the romantic adventures of our corny young lives. We cycled over to the café in Broad Haven and, as we parked the bikes, saw three girls going in.

'Nice looking, boy,' said Gus. 'Look at that one with the pony tail. She's great.'

All our preparatory dreams brewed headily within us: unattainable girls from Swansea or Cardiff, and wild ideas of their sophistication, guiding us skilfully into impossible amours. We were both, I suspect, slightly alarmed at the prospect and half-inclined to settle for somebody steady from Haverfordwest, but we didn't let on to each other.

There were strains of juke-box music wafting out on to the sea-front. The air was tingling with the sea-smells that had our hopeful senses jangling with a mixture of expectancy and panic. The music was pure syrup, rich, dark and lovely, a sort of cry-in-your-Coke country-and-western song, the sort of thing to madden any 16-year-old country boy with dreams of American mid-West farmers' daughters, sophistication and rich country pleasures rolled into one. We paused outside the door, very nervous now, because the great adventure began here. We went in.

It was a beautiful evening, in a tormented sort of way. We sat at one table, the three girls at another, a courting couple sniggered in the corner, and an old man who seemed to know the owner and have nowhere else to go sat in a cloud of pipe smoke by the door, passing the odd comment about the juke-box.

The girl with the pony-tail *was* great. This was the age of the pony tail and the suntan, and she really was the country-and-western dream, hair streaming as she galloped on horse-back through my fevered imagination, or spun in a gingham dress through the mazes of a barn dance. I'd just seen the film of 'Oklahoma!' This was Martha and she really was Miss 1958. She was perfect, and I feared very much that she was beyond me, but went on dreaming just the same.

We did our best to start what our earnest minds pictured as a conversational rush. Gus fixed them with a weak grin and let fall a remark, unbelievable in its triteness, about meeting nice girls like them in a place like that. But they must have been used to this sort of banter in their own town, because they laughed politely and responded in kind. We kept up a fair conversation for quite a while on this level of crunching mediocrity, before we switched to the intelligent-discussion tack, considering the pros and cons of each record, for most of which Gus and I were paying, with rippling remarks like, 'Yeah. It's got a great beat,' each sharp judgment of this kind being pushed out to sage nods. It was a lovely evening. We didn't take them home or anything, granted, but we had just over a fortnight in hand and we knew our place.

We cycled back to the tent slowly, bemused by this vision of the bright sophisticated world east of Whitland. I think they were from Cefneithin or Llandybie or somewhere, but that, to us, was 'Swansea way' and made them virtually unattainable, giving us all the more reason for giving chase. We had no clearcut strategy—there were three of them and two of us for a start, and we both wanted Martha—but we had all the dreams in the world.

'Better keep those jam jars out of sight,' mumbled Gus, as we were about asleep. 'She'd think we were a right couple of dicks if she saw us fishing for seaweed.'

'Yeah, I suppose so.' I was sorry about that. I'd planned an extensive operation for the following morning. 'What'll we do?'

'In the morning? Play football.' That made sense.

We went back to the café every night after that, and we used to see the girls occasionally on the beach while we were hamming up a tremendous exhibition of footballing skills. Our conversations in the café were developing to the pitch where we did actually start to talk sense with them once in a while, and we'd about reached the point where I was considering introducing our jam jars into the conversation, when suddenly, everything fell through. The holiday season seemed to start with a rush, and, the first weekend we were there, a crowd arrived, including Dev and the Swansea boys, and it was all ruined.

Let's just say of Dev that he was the big guy and he took over. He was with three mates and they genuinely did come from Swansea. They were footballers in a big way, those four, and somebody said that Dev was on Swansea Town's books as an apprentice professional. I don't know if that was true or not, because he was the sort of character who'd manage to *convince* everybody of something like that. Either way, he looked the part. He used to flash about the beach with a discarded Swansea Town shirt over his trunks and some flashy Adidas beach shoes, flicking up a much better ball than the one we were kicking around in our sloppy old daps. Then he had this habit, every time he called for the ball, which he did almost all the time, of calling the other boy 'son'. 'Right, son. Through ball.' 'In the air, son. Float it.' 'Run it, son, on your own.' That 'son' habit is a big one with Swansea Town players, so maybe he really was on their books.

He was a big lad, Dev, about a year older than Gus and me, I'd imagine, but brawny. Gus and I were small. Dev was good-looking in a repulsive sort of way, with a semi-crewcut, a Tony Curtis kiss-curl, and short sideboards, which in 1958 were mildly daring. In fact if Martha was Miss 1958, he was *Mr* 1958, which was a pretty lousy thing to be. And he started to treat Martha as his own personal property from the start.

We were in the café one evening, the night before the weekly hop in the church hall. Quite a crowd was already there, when Dev swanked in on a waft of aftershave. Gus was by the juke-box.

'What are you putting on, son?' he asked. 'Let's have "Manhattan Spiritual".' He leered round the tables. 'I like that. I'm very spiritual.' He grinned at Martha. 'Isn't that right, darling?' She smiled. 'Come outside the dance for half-an-hour tomorrow night and we'll have a spiritual get-together.'

He really did talk like that. I know Gus and I had talked drivel the previous few evenings, but at least we were bad at it. It's when something is both tripey *and* well done that it gets unpleasant. And, fair play, we were only corny, when all's said and done.

When Martha and her friends left, they just nodded, to our immense relief, and said 'See you again' when Dev offered to walk them home. But Dev leered round the café and said, 'She'll go, son. You wait.' We had the nasty feeling that he might try something on Martha, and we just hoped like hell that she wouldn't want anything to do with him. But he and Martha were out of the dancehall for about ten minutes the next night, even if Dev was looking a bit disgruntled when they came back in and, again, didn't walk her home. And all we got from the girls *we* danced with us, 'Dev's a case, isn't he? Isn't he handsome?' We were ready to crawl back to the tent and heave.

The second week of our fortnight was a bad one. There were a couple of dozen of us camped in Little Haven and every afternoon it was Dev's game which dominated the beach. 'Short ball, son. Roll it. Come on, son. In the air.' Big Dev, darting, sprinting, chesting down, etcetera. All the bag of tricks. Fair play, he *could* play football. Martha and her friends used to sunbathe on the pebbles in a central spot, directly overlooking Dev's game. Gus and I were reduced to rolling short, clumsy passes in a quiet corner. And every night in the café, Dev's laugh, everybody being called 'son' or 'darling', and Martha smiling all the while.

We used to plan Dev's ultimate downfall in the tent at night, plan to cut off his kiss-curl in his sleep and put it with seaweed in one of our jars, or plan to get the police to impound his Swansea Town shirt as stolen property. And as the week moved towards the final Saturday dance in the church hall, I told Gus that I would just like to walk into the dance holding Martha's hand, walk round the room, dance a couple of times and walk out again. 'A spiritual elopement' was the phrase I used. Just to shake Dev. But we'd given up. She'd been playing hard to get, but she'd go with him on the last night. But who cared? The whole big idea of great romances had gone sour on us long before the fortnight was up.

'The hell with it,' I said to Gus on the Friday night. 'Tomorrow morning I'm getting the jam jars out. And with any luck I'll put Dev in one and pickle him.'

It was a lovely morning, that Saturday, and I fried up before Gus had woken. By eight, I was down on the beach with a saddle bag full of jars, had found a little pool away in the corner and was on my own for over an hour, collecting everything, every kind of worm and fish and crab, all the seaweeds, arranging and re-arranging. I had a lovely time. Then I heard a voice.

'Hello, Adrian. What are you doing?'

It was Martha. I felt rather silly.

'I'm collecting seaweed.'

'Can I look?'

She looked at my two full jars. 'They're lovely. Look at those colours. Look at that little pink piece of seaweed there. It's like a ribbon. What a smashing hobby. Have you been doing it long?'

'Since about eight o'clock.'

'No, I meant, how long? You know, how many years?'

'Oh. Yes. For years. Gus and I live very near here, you see. We've been coming down since we were kids. We've always liked collecting them, but we've never known much about them.' Then, a bitter thought. 'We meant to do quite a bit of collecting this past fortnight but we never seemed to get around to it.'

'What a shame. I'd have loved to have come and watched you. Show me. With that one.'

I was away then. 'Well look. I usually start with the odd pebble. I'll take these home, you see, and keep them in the shed. The pebble will get covered with mossy stuff in time. All these things are alive, you see, and breed. Well, then, I add a little pool water, not too much, because quite a bit splashes in with the weeds and the animals . . .'

We had a marvellous morning. Dev and his crowd were playing football in the background, and Gus was watching from the pebbles, half jealous, but chiefly chuffed at seeing Dev become the victim of my brilliant spiritual elopement. By midday, I had filled all of my six jars.

'Can I finish one off?' asked Martha.

'Sure.'

'Just with one of these little pink pieces. Isn't it delicate? Look at the way the water fluffs it out.'

'It's a great hobby. Will you come to the dance with me tonight?'

There was a slight embarrassed pause, then she smiled. 'Yes, I'd like to. I'm going shopping with the girls in Haverfordwest this afternoon. What time shall I meet you?'

'Half past seven? Outside the café?'

She frowned. 'Has it got to be the café? I've been fed up these last two weeks with listening to records and people shouting at football.'

'I'll meet you just outside, if you like. Then we could go for a walk around the Point.'

'Yes. I'll see you at half past seven then. Just *outside* the café.'

She helped me carry the jam jars back up to my bike. Dev went on with his game.

I'd been fed up too, with records and football and Dev's talk in the café, but the walk I had with Martha around the Point made me feel better, was like one great big breath of fresh air. We talked of . . . well, simple things, like what we were doing at school, our families, tennis, which we both liked. We exchanged addresses and promised to write.

Then we went to the dance, really lifted up. Martha was a marvellous dancer; she jived like a young foal, her pony tail flying. We were really happy.

Dev arrived a bit drunk, later on. And everything happened quickly after that. He barged in, grabbed Martha's arm and said, 'Okay, son, I'll take over,' and I said, 'Like hell you will. She's with me.' Then there was a scrambly sort of scrap, with the Swansea boys and Gus and some of the boys from school joining in, and the vicar rushing in and out shouting, 'Come on now, boys, play the game,' and finally picking on me, the smallest, and saying, 'You're the troublemaker. Out you go,' and shoving me out into the street. I sat outside on the pavement, feeling a bit sick, worrying about Martha. Then she arrived, about the same time as Gus.

'Are you all right, Adrian?' she asked. 'That *was* brave, that really was. He was much bigger than you.'

'I'm okay.'

'Shall I walk back to your tent with you? I'll make you some tea.' She looked at Gus. 'Will that be all right?'

'Sure,' said Gus, who was past taking in any more. He went back into the hall.

We walked up the hill slowly, and Martha kept squeezing my arm and saying, 'That *was* brave, really.' Other than that, we didn't say much—we were holding hands and were both trembling a little. Even after we'd reached the tent and Martha had made some tea, we still didn't say a great deal. We talked a little, again, of schools and tennis; again, we promised to write to each other.

I was sharply conscious of Martha at moments only—mainly of the scent of femaleness about her. But generally, I was most aware of something rather different: the great hush out in the haven, and in the bay beyond. We sat holding hands for over an hour, before I finally walked her back to her caravan.

That summer seems a long way away now. Some things I still remember vividly. I remember very well the excited and expectant tingle of the sea front outside the café, as Gus and I *prepared* for the great adventure. I remember Dev, who seems fixed like a caricature, a cardboard man, in a remembered heat. And Martha . . . it's strange. I don't retain even a clear visual memory of her; in my mind's eye she blurs a little now with the film of 'Oklahoma!' Oddly, what I remember best are the seaweeds, pink, brown, floating, tingling with salt and sea water; anemones, starfish and sea beasts; and the moss, clinging to the tiny pebbles—darkening and growing rich.

Entertaining Sally Ann

I

I doubt very much if you're going to believe this. Husband, in early middle age, is instructed by wife and mother-in-law to pick up an attractive girl of twenty-four at the airport and to drive her back to Pembrokeshire. He has particularly strict instructions not to be back until well on into the second day, so is earnestly requested to spend a night with the girl in an exclusive country hotel in Powys (all expenses paid by mother-in-law).

Do me a favour, you say. This is middle-aged fantasising gone berserk. But hear me out. To appreciate the situation, you need to know more of the curious relationship between Gwyndaf, the dreamy historian, and his wife Cynthia, the latter being much abetted in all things by her mother, they two being specialists in the silvery laugh.

Cynthia and Mother-in-law are very much a part of what is known in Wales as the crachach. Their lives revolve around the Hunt Ball and similar well-oiled social functions, for which reason Mother-in-law has always looked on Cynthia's marriage to Gwyndaf as a low-key social disaster. Gwyndaf is on the one hand an Oxford graduate, which is something, but remains obstinately a history teacher, a rather un-crachach-like occupation. Moreover, his Gwendraeth Valley origins have left him with a dismissive lack of regard for social nicety, the ability barely to tell a red wine from a rosé, and a penchant for spending his leisure hours browsing in the deeper recesses of the history of Tudor Wales. Repeated efforts by Cynthia and Mother-in-law to buoy up Gwyndaf's social being have foundered on the bedrock of the historian's stubbornly dreamy and preoccupied nature. Cynthia's idea of social life is one of sparkling tinsel, a background against which she can ring out a silvery laugh and simulate flirtations with eligible young and not-so-young men ('eligible', in this case, encompassing solicitors, accountants, men in business, but not history teachers). It is all very harmless—dare one say it is a little vapid?—but it is a way of life in which Cynthia has been both groomed and, later, supported, by the peals of silvery laughter echoing back from her mother.

It is March, and diaries are being checked. Cynthia and Gwyndaf's mother-in-law have a problem. Mother-in-law has a friend, an old boarding-school-in-Berkshire friend, who emigrated many years ago to the U.S.A. and lives now in one of the grander suburbs of St Louis. The friend's daughter, Sally Ann, a single girl in her mid-twenties, has long harboured a desire to visit Wales, so mother-in-law has said she absolutely must come to Pembrokeshire to stay with them. Fine. Girl due at Heathrow early on the morning of Tuesday the 6th of May. Right on cue, Gwyndaf is due to drive back that day from London, where he will have been attending a conference of history teachers. But only in mid-March does mother-in-law realise that she and Cynthia are away in early May, making up a little party which is spending a few days in Ireland. They are due back mid-morning on Wednesday the 7th. This will never do. Mother-in-law absolutely must be there to receive the girl. It would be possible for Gwyndaf to entertain the girl overnight in his and Cynthia's house, but people do talk, of course, and such an arrangement could give rise to the most unseemly gossip. The trip to Ireland is too, too tempting to be put off. What is to be done?

'Suppose,' says mother-in-law ruminatively, 'suppose that Gwyndaf were to bring the girl back rather slowly?'

'Slowly?' says Cynthia. 'Mother. Gwyndaf drives slowly, I know, he dithers at junctions, but even Gwyndaf can't take a day-and-a-half to get down from Heathrow.'

'Darling,' says mother-in-law. 'A sight-seeing journey. He could show her sights, the English countryside, he could entertain her. And we could book them into a hotel a little out of their way. Powys somewhere. That's about a hundred miles north of the motorway. Yes. Some nice little country club in Powys. I know a couple. That's what we must do.'

'Mother,' says Cynthia. 'Gwyndaf will be furious. He hates entertaining people. And really, Mother, he can be so gauche, so awful. Gwyndaf can be awful in hotels. Usually he doesn't tip at all, and at other times he tips too much. He gets his orders muddled and confuses people. He really will hate it.'

'That's as may be, darling. But Gwyndaf will have to swallow his scruples.'

A meditative pause, before Cynthia giggles into gentle, inquisitive life. 'Mother. What if Gwyndaf flirts with her? Outrageously, let us say?'

Mother eyes her amusedly. 'Darling. Really. Gwyndaf?' They giggle delightedly. Exeunt both, to peals of silvery laughter.

And so it is arranged.

II

He looked at me in a shy kind of way and said, 'You must be Sally Ann.'

'That's right,' I said. 'And, Hey, I thought, he's nice. He had a nice deep voice and that sort of silvery-grey hair around the temples you get with guys around forty. He wasn't very smartly dressed, he had an old sweater and denims, but he looked like a scholar, with glasses, a deep, calm, soothing voice and a gentle smile. And I remember thinking, as we left the airport, This is an English gentleman.

Then, later, when he was telling me how to pronounce his name, with a 'v' sound at the end of 'Gwyndaf', and I noticed the rather nice, funny lilt in his voice, I thought, No, he's a Welsh gentleman. Not like the English ones you get in the movies, sharp, neat guys mostly, but a nice, dreamy, gentle sort of gentleman, in denims and a sweater. I figured I might enjoy our little trip.

I knew we were going down to Pembrokeshire over a day-and-a-half, which had seemed a little funny when Mom first told me, but she'd said distances seemed much farther in the U.K. And before long, Gwyndaf took the car off the highway and I saw what Mom had meant. We were traveling through these lovely fields and villages and pasture and farmland, and Gwyndaf, my gentleman friend, was telling me all about the buildings. Now who would have thought of that? A guy drives you in his car and he talks about the buildings you pass. But the big thing was that a whole lot of these buildings are what are called mock-Tudor (and they were cute, I liked them), but Gwyndaf said come tea time (and he really did use that phrase: 'tea time'), come tea time, we'd be in Shrewsbury and he'd show me some regular Tudor buildings. He was into Tudor things, he told me, he was a historian, for God's sake. Alright, I thought, not every girl gets to be driven round by a Welsh historian.

Then I think I worried a while. What did he think of me? I figured he'd find me attractive, that's no problem. I mean, I'm not too bad to look at. I weigh round a hundred and forty pounds, just a little big maybe, but my hair is long and smooth and is a nice chestnut kind of color. I have quite a good body, nice firm boobs and my hips are round and good. Okay, I'm just a little big, but I'm quite nice to look at. And, come on, it's not just looks. I think I have a nice personality.

Then Gwyndaf told me we'd be stopping at Oxford. We'd have lunch—'a meal', he called it—and then look at some of the colleges. And then he told me he'd been at one of these colleges himself. Then I really did worry. Would I be smart enough to keep this guy happy for a day-and-a-half? I'm a graduate, okay, but with a business degree from a college in Webster Groves, Missouri. And this guy was a graduate of Oxford University. But then I thought, Well no, what the heck, I majored in business admin and I'm holding down a job as a buyer with a big department store in St Louis. I can be smart as well as nice.

And then we got to Oxford. We had lunch and then we walked round a few colleges. We went to Gwyndaf's old college, Jesus College, and hey, he knew the janitor (or porter, he was called), this incredibly old guy in what he called the lodge out front, and they kidded back and forth for a while (well not really 'kidded'—they were quite grave and nice) and then we went out into this really great quadrangle, with its lawn and all these cute little staircases leading off to the rooms and studies. Only as soon as I thought that I checked myself. 'Come on, Sally Ann,' I thought, 'you can't think words like "cute". That's a real loud, brash American kind of thing to say. This is Oxford University, and the buildings are just so lovely to look at.' And they were. How many people get to be shown around a lovely old college like that by a guy who's a graduate there?

Then we went on and looked at other colleges and buildings, and he told me what parts were the oldest and which were the Tudor ones. Wadham College was a Tudor one, I remember. This Tudor was obviously a big thing with him, and that was good, because I minored in British and American lit in college and I knew something about the Tudors (like about Henry Eighth and Queen Elizabeth) so I could keep the show going quite nicely.

And then, after a while, when we'd driven out of Oxford, it was like I was drifting off into a kind of dream. This was all Tudors and the past and countryside, and a deep dreamy voice easing me along. We drove on to Shrewsbury, through just endless fields and villages, and through some place (Evesham, maybe?) where there were apple orchards and this gorgeous pink and white blossom.

And then we got to Shrewsbury, at tea time. And we really did have tea, lemon tea, in a little quaint old place called a 'tea room'. But it seemed like Gwyndaf was busting a gut to get me back out into the streets in Shrewsbury and to show me more buildings. He was an eager kind of a guy that way. Which was nice, it really was.

Now Shrewsbury has these really wild Tudor buildings. The mock-Tudor ones we'd driven past earlier, back in Berkshire or some place, they were quite elegant, but these were . . . as I said, wild. They were as if they were damn near crumpled up, all squished in around the rooves, and leaning over. This was the real past now, this was really good. And . . . oh, there were so many other things he had to show me. There was the old town clock . . . and hey, I thought I had something there. One of our set texts when I minored in lit was Henry Fourth, Part One, and there's a line there about Shrewsbury clock. And that really excited Gwyndaf when I told him (like, you could see him thinking, Gee, this girl is smart), only it turned out that this was a later clock. Gwyndaf fixed the date on it, later than Shakespeare, by reading off the Roman numerals, the way these guys do.

And then we walked beside the river a while, and watched guys rowing. There's some grand kind of a school there, I guess, and guys go on to Oxford and the other old university, Cambridge, and row there.

Then, later, around six, we crossed the border into Wales (only it was odd, because we crossed it, then went back into England for a while, then crossed it again). And this was Powys, this was Wales, and we'd be stopping soon for the night.

I don't think that Gwyndaf had been to that hotel before, but it turned out to be an old Tudor mansion, so he was excited right away. He was very relaxed now and happy, and that made me happy too, because I thought, Well, he can't find me too bad to be with. We sat in the big room there, by this big crackling log fire, and he had a good snoop round at the paintings in the room, portraits mainly. Portraits were fashionable with the Tudors, he told me.

Then a bartender came round to our corner and said there'd be some dancing in the dining room that night. The dining room had a little ballroom area and a combo was due in that night, three guys, a pianist, a bass man and a drummer. And we thought, Wow (like, both of us thought that), Wow, let's go for it. I had a ball gown packed away in my small valise, and Gwyndaf said he'd packed a suit for dinner, so that was great. We chatted and I asked him if he was a regular dancer, which he wasn't, but neither was I, so we figured we'd shuffle round together. And then we were off to change for our dinner-dance.

I was glad I had that ball gown when I met him at dinner. It's not too low in front (for I'd have hated him to think I was cheap), but it leaves my arms and shoulders bare. My arms and shoulders are my best feature, I guess. I have a nice smooth skin and people have commented on how nice I look with my shoulders bare.

Then, at dinner, Gwyndaf said something that puzzled me. He said he wasn't very good with people in hotels. I couldn't see that. With all the other people we'd met that day, like the old porter in Jesus College and even the people in the tea room at Shrewsbury, he'd been fine—happy and natural. But he said now he didn't know much about wines and stuff like that, except he did know you had white wine with poultry and red wine with red meat, and that was all. So, we were having beef, so what say we asked for red wine? That was fine by me.

Afterwards, I danced close to him. Not too close (as I say, I didn't want him to think me cheap or slinky—for I'm not). It's just that it had been a lovely day, and he was a real Welsh gentleman, and I wanted him to know I felt warm and nice about him. So just now and again I nuzzled up against him a little. Not too often, just now and again. A girl knows how to judge these things.

And the last thing was, just after midnight, we separated in the corridor leading off to my room. And he took my hand (can you believe this?) and he squeezed it just a little, then he raised it to his lips and gave it a very gentle kiss. That really was too much. I was very close to tears. What a lovely courteous thing to do.

In my bedroom, I lay awake a long while, watching the moonlight shine through a gap in the curtains. After a while, I got out of bed, and opened the curtains and peeped out. There was a warm lovely moonlight streaming down and all underneath were mountains and Powys and Wales. And then I went back to bed and fell asleep, dreaming of my lovely Tudor gentleman.

III

Even as we were getting introduced, and I said I was 'Gwyndaf' and not 'Gwyn-daff', I sensed we'd get on well together. She was a bright and cheerful girl, she'd read a little Shakespeare, and she really did make me feel that taking her round Oxford and Shrewsbury had been the right thing to do.

And of course, my vanity—and maybe it wasn't just my vanity—was touched, because she really was a beautiful woman. Or 'beautiful' to my taste—to a Tudor taste, if you like. She belonged in a different and more gracious age, before our present saturnalia, and slinky little floozies. She belonged to a time when women were thought of best if they were considered 'handsome'—or 'comely' even. I suppose the bare shoulders revealed by her ball gown were at odds with the Tudor fashion for ruffs and high necklines, but that ballroom was no place to be pedantic. In her ball gown she was a picture. Her shoulders were bare, save for the lovely chestnut tresses flowing over them. Her arms too were bare and just slightly plump. She was a very handsome girl and it was a pleasure to be with her.

There is just the one intriguing little postscript. A day or so after Sally's and my return, Cynthia and Mother-in-law quizzed me about our trip. They conceded that Oxford and Shrewsbury had been quite good choices, and seemed deeply relieved that I'd ordered a red wine to go with the beef. Then mother-in-law hopped into life.

'And what about the country club? Was it one of their ballroom evenings?'

'Oh, yes.'

'You danced with her, I hope?' said Cynthia. 'You didn't leave her sitting out like a gooseberry?'

'Oh, no,' I said. 'We danced. Right through, in fact. To close of play, as it were.'

Mother-in-law muttered approval. 'Well, it seems to have paid off. The girl can't speak too highly of you. She told me she had a lovely trip.' They both nodded at me, bemusedly, as if still a little baffled at my social coup. 'Well done, Gwyndaf,' said the perplexed mother-in-law.

Well done. My mind was far away: on Oxford, Shrewsbury, Tudor buildings, apple blossom at Evesham, Powys in the moonlight, a crackling log fire and bare white shoulders. Well done indeed.

An April Story

She is so obviously the classic innocent, a brown sepia image, the type and representative of all our yesterdays. But let us fill the empty spaces, gather her coming century around her, build a fiction...

Haverfordwest, Market Street, 1906...
The print, a brown sepia photograph, has been on my wall for some time. Superficially, it is pastoral. There is no vehicle to be seen, save for a horse and cart at the top end of the street. Foreground, a cluster of small boys and bigger boys stands, with caps and breeches, hands in pockets, feigning a nonchalance towards the camera which they are still eyeing furtively. And right up foreground is a girl of perhaps fourteen, with a broad-brimmed hat, a bright white blouse, spruce black stockings, a shopping basket and a skirt whose hem is just slightly uneven. She gazes at the camera much more firmly and intently than the boys.

Large Victorian (and older) buildings frame our view. Commerce House stands massively, a 1906 department store, behind the girl. A shoe shop has a jumble of its wares hung outside it. And, halfway up the street, is Brigstocke's printing works, already publishing a weekly newspaper. It is a busy town. But in a way of course they are innocent— innocent of two world wars, of Fascism and international Communism, of Thatcherism and the Internet.

The little girl, foreground. What are her hopes and expectations? Let us create her story, start to build a fiction. Let us say she is fourteen, that her name is Louise and that the month is April. It makes good sense to say it could be April, for it is bright enough to take a photograph, yet cool enough for the boys at any rate to be dressed quite warmly. But, for Louise's sake and for the sake of the story which we shall build for her, let it certainly be April. She is coming into life and leaf and April is a good month for setting out.

She gazes quite intently at the camera, arms wrapped around her shopping basket's handle, almost in a pose. There is no smile, but I suspect she is pleased to be caught thus by the camera and for her image to be preserved. She would hardly imagine though that the writer of this present memoir will gaze upon her and her Market Street with such wonderment and fascination, in ninety-three years' time.

Let us move rapidly now to fiction. She is a little stern in her expression, not just because of the camera, but because Benny the butcher's boy has bothered her again. Every Saturday morning, as she goes to Market Street for her mother's shopping, she is chivvied and annoyed by Benny, who delivers on Saturday morning for a High Street butcher. He will sneak up behind her and tweak and tug the long black tresses of her hair. Once he tried to kiss her. The other girls say he likes her and this morning she feels the mingling of a hot exasperation and an excitement which isn't quite driven out by the excitement of the camera. Despite both these excitements, she is sedate and ladylike. In time, she will marry Benny the butcher's boy, Ben Butch. For a year, he will be sent away to Swansea to work with a butcher-uncle and to learn his trade, while she works in a draper's shop. She will wait for him and they will marry in the spring of 1914.

* * *

It is going into February 1916 and Ben Butch has been in France now, with the Welsh Regiment, for over a year. He has been back just once, on a short sick leave, because of frostbite in his feet—they call it 'trench foot'. His is not a bad case, but Louise was horrified to see the puckering and to sense his pain. And then he recovered (at least partially) and returned to the front.

She is lonely. While Ben is away, she is living with her parents and can only hope for that 'one day' when he comes back and they will set up home together. For all that, there are still things to do and, occasionally, places to go. She still has her job in the draper's shop and a little money, but ekes it out warily, spending a little on clothes and (regularly) on trips to the picture palace. She goes regularly to Bethesda chapel, where there will be a social next Thursday and the Annual Tea and Concert in March. Last Sunday the pastor gave what seemed to have been an important sermon (for the local newspaper reported it at length) on 'God's Trust in Man', but Louise's mind was half-attending; filling her thoughts was the prospect of a new production at the picture palace the following week: a play, a real play, not a picture, with eighteen artists, a play called 'The Broken Rosary'. She loved it, loved the glitter and the escape.

Some things she can only dream about. There will be the dance soon at the Assembly Rooms, where the dancing will not start till eight and there will be dancing and cards till the early hours. But that will be for the gentry really, and anyway it will cost two-and-six.

She contributes though (and this is her one very earnest, if rather helpless-feeling contribution to the war effort) to the local cigarette fund, so that her pennies, her threepences and the occasional sixpence will help towards packets of cigarettes to be sent to the boys at the front. She reads in the newspaper of how grateful the boys are. 'My chums and I settled down to a really grand smoke,' said one, and she is pleased to have contributed something. Ben Butch smokes. Perhaps some of her contributions will make their way to him.

The newspaper is sometimes a worry though. She reads of the deaths of local boys, of amputation, and the dreaded 'trench foot'. But their spirits are high—only sometimes Louise is uneasy about how high their spirits are. One local soldier (whom again she read about in the newspaper—the paper is so full of war news) was sent back on sick leave with damaged eyesight, but just said that a shell had exploded 'unpleasantly near'. She is frightened by the heartiness and afraid for them. Afraid for Ben Butch—and for herself.

One edition of the newspaper had a strange story of a senior army officer who is being court martialled at Scoveston fort for drunkenness. Louise just wonders what all the fuss is about. There is drunkenness in town every night.

Remember: this is a fiction, Louise's April story. So I could tell you now that Louise will hear, later that year, that Ben Butch has been killed in action. He will have died a brave death and been a credit to his regiment.

But our story will not tell you that. The writer of this fiction wants happiness for Louise and was moved and touched by the sense of hope and radiance which emanated from her in 1906. So Benny Butch will live. He will return, he will set up home with Louise just after Christmas 1918, and their two sons, Gareth and Robert, will be born in 1919 and 1922.

* * *

The nineteen-twenties are wonderful. Ben Butch is back home, one of the lucky ones, unscathed save for a bad limp, and by 1926 he has set up his own butcher's shop in Bridge Street. The four of them live over the shop.

The twenties, going on into the thirties, are the era of Louise's young motherhood and she is glad that she and her sons have Bridge Street and the town, with all their noise and excitement. Rising elegantly at the end of the street is the Swan Hotel, a coaching inn, which has a yard where horses are stabled. There is the clatter of hooves every morning and the older boys run after the horses, asking if they can hold a horse's head for the farmers who clatter in. They get sixpence usually for this service. Louise will always remember the day when Gareth, her elder boy, rushes home, flushed and excited, to announce that he has just held a horse's head. Louise loves such things. She mothers the boys with humour and humanity.

There are many other sounds: the milkmen shouting 'Milko!' and the rattle of their churns; sheep bleating as they are brought to the mart; the clang of the hammer on the anvil from the blacksmith's shop in Holloway; the cocklewomen up from Llangwm, the chip carts; every Saturday, music on the Castle Square, the Boys' Brigade bugle band, the Salvation Army.

And rich deep smells. The curious smell of the horses being hooved. The smells of their butchers' shop, of cheese and soap from the groceries and the hot bread smell from the bakeries and cake shops. Best of all perhaps is the smell of roasting chestnuts, crackling in their braziers on cold winter evenings. In October, there is Portfield Fair . . .

* * *

The nineteen-thirties are a mellow time. Ben's business does well and they are earning enough now to send the boys to the grammar school, where both do well. In 1937, Gareth will leave town, in term time, for the teacher training college in Cheltenham. Twice, the rest of the family go up to visit him and Louise is intrigued by the vista of such a large and gracious town. Otherwise, they travel very little; their holidays are to Tenby or the Gower coast.

There is plenty in town which they enjoy. Not only is there the Palace Cinema now, but the new County Theatre at which, on one memorable night, soon after the theatre has opened, they hear a performance by Paul Robeson. Louise has never met or seen a Negro before and has an excited sense that the town is moving now to some greater familiarity with the world beyond. They go to the pictures very often; Louise would love to go to dances too, but this cannot be because of the legacy of Ben's trench foot.

Louise's first sight of Adolf Hitler is on a newsreel at the Palace and she watches later newsreels with the same mixture of disbelief and amusement. He seems a comic foreigner, a Charlie Chaplin figure, jabbering and gesticulating, and she cannot take seriously those people who talk of the threat of another war. In time however, she feels a little knot of tension tightening in her stomach. Surely, surely, it cannot happen again. Surely not. When she sees on the Palace screen the picture of Mr Chamberlain, returned from Munich and his talks with Herr Hitler, waving his paper and saying it is 'peace in our time', Louise is exultant. She clutches tightly to Ben's arm in the darkened cinema and is literally weeping tears of joy. She feels she could not have faced another war. Then come the annexations of the Sudetanland and Poland—then war. Louise is numbed with disbelief. First Gareth and then Robert are called up.

* * *

Louise finds war even harder the second time around. She has Ben Butch beside her now, which makes for comfort, but at night sometimes she can feel him twisting and muttering in his sleep and she knows that he, like her, is plagued by dreams of two sons overseas and at war. Gareth is on a minesweeper; Robert in the infantry.

Life goes on of course, but the daily round of the butcher's shop is not the pleasure it was in peacetime. There is rationing for one thing and they are often beset by customers who would hope for more than their fair share, who would hope that Ben could somehow conjure a little extra. They earn less of course, but Louise doesn't care about that. Her mind is on her two boys, overseas. Letters arrive from them occasionally, but they are an odd mixture of the laconic and the jolly and Louise doesn't really trust them. The action had been 'pretty hellish', Gareth said once, but 'the boys are bearing up pretty well'. Louise is afraid of censorship, afraid that something awful has happened (or will happen) to her sons. And yet she knows that, like everyone else, must must be cheerful and get on with things and be proud of the fact that her sons are serving their country. Never before has she wished she'd had daughters, but she sometimes wishes that now. Yet nothing will erase the constant recollection of her two sons, so far away, so young.

The war at home is cruel too, on times. There are air raid sirens, with their eerie wail; there is heavy bombing in Swansea and, once, in Pembroke Dock. But all the time it is her sons' plight which leaves Louise most frightened.

She and Ben go the Palace and the County still, they love the cinema, even though the trudge to get there through the blacked-out streets is rather sad. Lately they've seen Errol Flynn in 'Virginia City' and James Cagney with Pat O'Brien in 'Boy Meets Girl'. Louise has grown to love American things and still cherishes the recollection of hearing Robeson sing, even though she never has been (and never will go) to America. There are dances still, run by the dairy students, the Home Guard, all manner of people, and you can get in for two or three shillings. She would so love to go and feels that dancing might really help to lift her spirits, but with Ben's trench foot that is impossible. Once though, they do go to a dance, run by the Home Guard, in which Ben is a corporal. He and Louise go along and she can dance with his friends. It's not the same as dancing with Ben would be, but she still finds the music and the movement a kind of comfort.

Louise could hear, in 1943 or 1944, that either or both of her sons is missing, presumed dead. But this fiction will not do that to her. It is clear of course, given the manifold cruelties of her and our century, that such a thing could happen. But it will not. Gareth and Robert will survive. This is partly charity. The writer of this fiction has come by now to admire Louise's resilience and decency, has grown indeed very fond of her, and wishes for her a happy outcome.

VE Night is ecstatic. The streets are thronged and lit again, there are cheering and singing which last until the early morning. Louise and Ben both get very drunk, something they're not really used to, and Louise is sick on the way home. But it just doesn't matter. She knows now, is sure, her sons will soon be back and safe.

* * *

We move into the post-war world. Mr Churchill warns of an Iron Curtain coming down over Europe, and the first atomic bombs have been exploded in Hiroshima and Nagasaki. In the euphoria of the boys' return, Louise barely notices.

But now? Oddly, as we move on, post-war, Louise becomes ever more shadowy and enigmatic, the strands of her story more difficult to gather. What will she know and feel and experience?

She will have (and has had) what are sometimes known, with either sentiment or derision (and quite falsely either way) as the simple things in life: a husband and two sons who have survived the two Great Wars; good health; grandmotherhood, robust and roseate. She will never travel to America but she has savoured so much of what is about her: the moment when her elder son came home to boast of how he had held a horse's head and been given sixpence; fairs and festivals and roasting chestnuts; the smell of bread from cake shops; thronged streets, hot Christmasses, the returning warmth of spring. Our April story wants all that for her, not because it seeks to be sentimental or unreal, but because this fiction is suffused with the feeling that the simplest lives, if allowed to carry through, unimpeded and unbereaved, can indeed be magical.

The little girl gazes out, sedate, inscrutable, from her photograph of 1906.

Biographical Notes

Glenda Beagan is a native of Rhuddlan, the landscape of the surrounding North Wales area featuring prominently in her work. She studied with the Open University before gaining a First Class Honours in English at Aberystwyth, followed by an MA in Creative Writing at Lancaster. She has published two volumes of short stories, *The Medlar Tree* and *Changes and Dreams*, both published by Seren, and a collection of her poetry, *Vixen*, was published by Honno. Her work has been widely anthologised, most notably in *The Green Bridge* (ed. John Davies) and in *The New Penguin Book of Welsh Short Stories* (ed. Alun Richards).

Leonora Brito was born and brought up in Cardiff. Her stories have been included in anthologies published by Viking/Penguin, Sheba, Seren and Parthian. Her collection of short stories, *Dat's Love*, was published by Seren in 1995.

Gillian Clarke was born in Cardiff. She has published seven collections of poetry. Her work is studied for GCSE and A level in Wales and England. She teaches on the Creative Writing M.Phil. course at the University of Glamorgan. Recent collections of poems include *Collected Poems* (Carcanet 1997) and *Five Fields* (Carcanet 1998), *Nine Green Gardens* (Gomer 2000) and a collection for children, *The Animal Wall and Other Poems* (Pont Books 1999). She lives in Ceredigion.

Jo Hughes was born in Swansea in 1956. Her stories have appeared in a number of magazines and anthologies and have been broadcast on Radio 4. She was one of the winners in the Rhys Davies Competition in both 1995 and 1999. She is currently working on her first novel.

Mike Jenkins was born in Aberystwyth. He has lived and taught in Merthyr Tudful for over twenty years. He is a former editor of *Poetry Wales* and is a co-editor of *Red Poets Society*, a magazine of socialist poetry. His book of interlinked short stories, *Wanting to Belong,* won the Wales Book of the Year award (English section) in 1998. It was featured in the Channel 4 series *Writers from Wales* in May 2000. His new and selected poems *Red Landscapes* (Seren) was published in 1999.

Catherine Merriman is the author of four novels and two collections of short stories. Her first novel *Leaving the Light On* (Gollancz/Pan, 1992) won the Ruth Hadden Memorial Award and her first story collection *Silly Mothers* (Honno, 1991) was a runner-up for Welsh

Book of the Year. She has twice been a Rhys Davies Short Story Award prize winner. She lives near Abergavenny in Monmouthshire.

Robert Nisbet was born and brought up in Haverfordwest. After thirty years teaching English in secondary schools, he now tutors creative writing for the W.E.A. and at Trinity College, Carmarthen. He is the author of six collections of short stories, the most recent being *Entertaining Sally Ann* (Alun Books, 1997). An earlier collection, *Sounds of the Town* (Alun Books, 1982) was a runner-up in the Dylan Thomas Award competition in 1983. His stories have appeared frequently in literary quarterlies in the U.S.A. and have been translated into German and Romanian.